Mr. Potts & Me

The Power of Storytelling

Mr. Potts & Me

The Power of Storytelling

By Damon L. Fordham

EVENING POST BOOKS
Our Accent is Southern!
www.EveningPostBooks.com

Published by
Evening Post Books
Charleston, South Carolina
www.EveningPostBooks.com

Editors: John M. Burbage, Holly Holladay, Jamie Pohlman
Design: Gill Guerry

Photos

Cover: Walter Snype, late 1960s, courtesy of Ms. Karen Francis, granddaughter of Mr. Snype; Damon L. Fordham, 1972, provided by the author

Dedication page: Abraham Fordham, provided by the author

First printing 2012
Printed in the United States of America

A CIP catalog record for this book has been applied for from the Library of Congress.

ISBN: 978-0-9834457-6-0

Dedication

To the memory of
Walter "Pappa" Snype (1896-1973)

and to my dad,

Abraham Fordham (1922-1984),
who inspired the writing
of this book.

Acknowledgments

Special thanks to my mother, Pearl Fordham, for a number of these stories, my sister Bobbie for helping with the graphics, and John Coles and Alada Shinault Small for computer advice. Much love to all my friends and relatives in the Fordham, Francis, Brown, Johnson, Moore, Montgomery, McGowan, Howard, Collier, McDonald, Maxwell, Scott and Campbell families in Mt. Pleasant, St. Stephen and Spartanburg, S.C.

To my mentors Dean Willie Harriford (University of South Carolina), Joseph Kimpson (Carver High School, Spartanburg, S.C.), Carl Gathers (Mt. Pleasant Awareness Center), Brother Osei Chandler, LeGrand Wilson, the Rev. L.O. Johnson (1916-2002), the Rev. Joseph T. Jackson (1916-1987), Samuel McGowan (1933-2002) and Marvin Dulaney (College of Charleston), among many others: Thanks for finishing up where Dad left off. Special thanks to Birdie Sanders for encouraging my love for reading and writing, and the many young people I've had the pleasure of teaching and mentoring over the last 10 years. Thanks to my Aunt Barbara Collier, John Carr and

Mildred Seabrook Bobo for additional stories in this text.

Acknowledgements are also in order for those who reviewed this manuscript: Norman Nelson, Danielle Hardee, John Coles, Herb Frazier, Beverly Birch, Horace Mungin and Mark Tiedje. Thank you to Karen Francis, William Dudley Gregorie and Harlan Greene for some of the additional material.

Finally, to the love of my life, Jayne Wilson Roper, for bringing joy and laughter to my world, for proofreading this and for her unconditional love and support.

Prologue

Culture, tradition, humor and wisdom have been passed down by way of storytellers throughout history. This is especially true in the oral folk traditions of the Southern United States. Every family and town had individuals who entertained and educated with information of bygone days and accepted moral standards.

The days when the local teller of tales gathered those who cared to listen and shared his experiences are largely a thing of the past. Television and other forms of electronic media are major sources of information on which most people in the United States rely today. Many children never have experienced genuine storytelling from a wise adult.

I was fortunate that my father, Abraham Fordham, recognized the importance of storytelling. He was a school-teacher who entertained his students and adults with anecdotes, tall tales and historical information. During my childhood, he filled my mind with tales of his experiences during the Great Depression, World War II and the Civil Rights Movement.

I have preserved many of my father's tales and those of other elders through the fictional character of Mr. Ernest

Potts. Some incidents described in these pages are loosely based on those of my childhood. Others come from my imagination. I hope they encourage you to go to your elderly friends and relatives and write down their stories before their tales are lost. I hope this book inspires you to one day sit down and share the good things that you know with young people in your life.

Damon L. Fordham
February 2012
Mt. Pleasant, S.C.

Table Of Contents

In the Beginning

Lucinda Potts sang gospel songs while doing a little spring-cleaning in the living room of her Mount Pleasant home. The doorbell rang.

"Come on in. It's open."

The front door creaked wide and a young lady peeked in.

"Amelia! You all right?" Mrs. Potts asked.

Amelia Moore stepped into the house where she had been raised by Lucinda and Ernest Potts. She was not smiling. Her husband Robert died after a sudden heart attack only a week ago and she had not seen her foster mother for two days.

Mrs. Potts wrapped her thick brown arms around Amelia. "How's Luke holding up? Is he OK?"

Amelia was only 5 years old when Mr. and Mrs. Potts entered her life days after her parents passed away. Mr. and Mrs. Potts had heard about her situation from friends and did not hesitate to take Amelia in.

Amelia grew up happily and appreciative of their kindness. She married Robert Moore after an appropriate courtship, and soon they had a son whom they named Lucas.

He was just eight years old when his father passed away.

Mrs. Potts steered Amelia toward the couch. "I know this is hard, honey, but God is in control."

"Yes ma'am, I know."

"About Luke...you didn't say how he's taking it."

"I don't know what to do about him."

"What you mean, child?"

"I don't want to bother...."

"Now listen," Mrs. Potts said, "you're our daughter. Ernie and I love you. You're never a 'bother.' You're a blessing."

Amelia sighed and said, "Well, Luke needs a man as good as his daddy was...."

"Don't stop now, child," Mrs. Potts whispered.

"He needs a someone who'll teach him what being a man is all about, someone who'll set a good example. I have to work, and I can only do so much. Perhaps Mr. Potts could...."

"Of course, dear. Mr. Potts will be perfect. Aside from smoking that smelly pipe and telling them fool rabbit stories, Ernie is a fine example for that boy. And Luke is mighty fond of the old man already."

"Thank you," Amelia said. "May I ask Mr. Potts in person? Where is he anyway?"

"Out back where he always is this time of day — in the tool shed either fixing something that's broke or entertaining the usual crowd with those fool stories."

"Mr. Potts' stories aren't that bad," Amelia said.

"Trust me, after all of these years of listening to him,

those stories are wearin' thin," Mrs. Potts chuckled. "Come on, let's go find him."

• • •

The tool shed stood — leaned actually — in a corner of the back yard. The roof was rusty red tin and everything else was wood, except for the glass in the two big front windows. The building was illuminated inside by a bare light bulb in the ceiling. Its wooden walls were covered with hooks and nails on which hung an array of tools, appliance parts, fan belts, outdated feed-store calendars and whatnot. Half-quart canning jars full of nails, nuts, bolts and washers were each screwed into lids attached to the bottom of a shelf across the backside wall. A row of well-worn books lined the top of the shelf.

The shed had a cement floor and in the center stood a wood stove vented by a black stovepipe straight up through the roof. Several old stools and chairs were situated around the heater.

Ernest Monroe Potts — a bald, rather heavy-set man in his 70s — occupied the biggest chair in the circle. He wore black suspenders, a checkered flannel shirt, gray trousers and silver wire-framed eyeglasses. Six other men, each of them also seated comfortably, completed the gathering. Mr. Potts pretended he was fixing a broken alarm clock while swapping tales with his friends.

The door was opened slightly and as the ladies approached the shed they noted the aroma of assorted brands of tobacco and beer — in which some of the men indulged as they warmed themselves by the kerosene stove. Waves of laughter filled the room as a transistor radio provided a steady stream of rhythm and blues through the static. The ladies stopped near the entrance and observed.

"Let me ask y'all something," Ernest Potts boomed in a deep, full voice. "Y'all remember the colored theater over in Charleston?"

"Yeah," said James "King" White, a slender man sporting a bright red fedora. He was Mr. Potts' closest competition in the art of storytelling. "I remember that dirty louse-trap, and I ain' lying."

Old Joe Blunt remembered it too. "The screen was so filthy that even if they showed 'The Ten Commandments,' everybody inside worried about getting arrested for watching dirty movies!"

The men howled in unison at that.

"Now wait a minute," said Lucius Rouse, a light-complexioned gentleman with a receding gray hairline and dignified disposition. "The man who owned that place couldn't help how some of his customers messed it up. He was a good man, fed all the poor kids in the neighborhood every Christmas."

"Either way," Mr. Potts said, lighting his pipe and adjusting his glasses, "I watched the funniest cartoon I ever saw from the front row in that theater one day just after the war. It showed a man's house full of Christmas presents under the tree, and a voice in the background said:

'Twas the night before Christmas
And all through the house

Not a creature was stirring,
Not even a mouse.

"Then this rat popped his head out of a hole in the wall and told the audience, 'THAT'S WHAT YOU THINK!'"

The men slapped their legs and rocked back in their seats, hooting and hollering like they were watching a chicken fight.

The ladies laughed, too, but quietly as they continued to eavesdrop. "Mrs. Potts," Amelia whispered, "let's wait a few more minutes. I hate to interrupt him while he's on a roll."

Mrs. Potts smiled.

"Now of course," Mr. Potts continued as he took another puff from his pipe, "real life is fooler than them cartoons. What I'm saying is, fact is stranger than fiction. Take my cousin Charlie from way back in the country. He come to see Lucinda and me back in the late-1950s, and he said he was amazed at how we lived. Cousin Charlie was from so far back in the woods that he ain' never been in a house that had electricity. And he wasn't too bright either. When he walked into the living room, he started screaming, 'AAAAAAHHH…Ernie! Ernie! Come quick!'

"Me and Lucinda ran into the room. 'What's the matter, Charlie?' I asked.

"Well, that boy was standing there sweating like a hog with its eyes popping out like golf balls. 'Somebody 'bout to shoot somebody dead in here!' Charlie said.

"Fact of the matter is, Charlie had never seen TV before, and had come face to face with a shoot-'em-up cowboy show on our brand-new black-and-white set."

Then came another wave of laughter. They were almost settled back down when Hamp Fludd said, "Listen fellas, that ain't nothing. I know a fool fooler than that."

"That's a mighty big fool," Mr. Potts noted.

"Y'all remember Dodo, don't you?"

Everyone in the room nodded knowingly.

"Dodo drank up his paycheck like water in a glass," Hamp continued. "He once bet old-man Walker's boy that he could drink liquor faster than any man alive."

Then Hamp jumped up out of his chair and said:

"So the dummies got out there in the middle of the street each of them with a quart of whiskey sticking out the pockets of their pants like cowboys fixing to have a shootout. Somebody hollered 'Draw!' and both of them fools pulled out their bottles and drank as fast as they could — at the same time."

The howls and guffaws that followed shook the shed so hard that it leaned at least another two inches.

"Next thing you know," Hamp continued, "Dodo went down in the middle of the street like a sack of potatoes falling off a wagon, and they had to carry him home. They didn't realize until they got there that Dodo was as dead as a rusty doornail. So they sat him up in the chair at the table in his mama's kitchen just as the rigor mortis started setting in. And when his mama and daddy got home, they didn't think nothing was wrong with Dodo until they noticed he wasn't saying nothing at the dinner table."

The men chortled enthusiastically; the ladies feigned

disgust. And King White piped in:

"Man, that ain't nothing! Did I every tell you about that fool I knew back in Hoover time?"

"What's Hoover time?" Alfred Jackson asked. He was younger than the rest of them.

King White was not pleased by this interruption. "That was back during the Depression when Mr. Herbert Hoover was the President. You need to read a book about that man. You might learn something. And don't butt in when grown folks are talking.

"Anyway," King continued, "this fool I'm talking about was way out plowing a field and wiping sweat from his brow because it was real hot in the middle of the day, and he looked up at the clouds. Suddenly, he dropped the plow and commenced to jumping around like he just got religion.

"'Hallelujah! Praise the Lord!' he screamed until this old preacher they called The Prophet stopped while walking along the dirt road next to the field and hollered, 'What the hell is wrong with you?'

"Well, that fool out in the field looked back at the preacher and yelled back, 'I is washed with the blood of the Lamb and I is seen the light!'

"'You what?' The Prophet hollered.

"'That right. I was plowing hot and heavy and I looked up in the sky and saw three big letters in the clouds — G.A.P. — and I know exactly what that means: Go And Preach! So I quit all this plowing and sweating and being dragged round behind this mule. I'm gonna do exactly what the Good Lord told me to do!'

"Well, the old Prophet looked up in the sky and saw the three letters and shook his wrinkled head and responded: 'That don't say Go And Preach! That say Go and Plow!'"

The men in Mr. Potts' tool shed laughed heartily.

"Lord have mercy!" Mrs. Potts said to Amelia. "We must break this up or somebody might get hurt." She knocked on the door before swinging it open and stepping through the doorway. Everybody stopped what they were doing and looked at her.

"Ernest, may I see you for a moment?"

Dead silence.

Mr. Potts looked at Lucinda then around at his friends.

"Better get going, Mr. Potts," King White warned. "The boss is calling."

The men elbowed each other and snickered. Mr. Potts stood up and stared them all down. And as soon as all was quiet, Mrs. Potts said, "Ernie, I hate to interrupt while you're working, but Amelia here needs to talk to you."

The old man's face lit up at the sight of Amelia and out the door he went. The tool-shed session ended early this go round.

• • •

"Hello, cute self!" Mr. Potts said to Amelia as soon as the three of them got through the back door of the house and into the kitchen. "What can I do for you?"

Amelia explained the situation regarding Luke and her job.

The old man folded his left arm, and cupped his chin

between his thumb and first finger and asked, "I assume you already talked to Mrs. Potts about this?"

"Yes, sir."

"Well, between the two of you and my conscience, the majority rules. Cute self, starting tomorrow, have the boy come over here directly after school until you come get him after work."

Mrs. Potts and Amelia looked at each other with broad smiles.

The Tale-Telling Contest

Ernest Monroe Potts had a daily routine. He rose at 6:30 a.m. like he did before he retired from the Naval Shipyard in North Charleston. After breakfast with his wife, he read the *News and Courier*, then went back to the tool shed to work on various repair projects — mostly for his neighbors. He charged a small fee depending on their income.

At noon he returned to the house for lunch with his wife, unless she was at church, and went back to the shed at 3 p.m. when his friends arrived. Everyone knew his rules.

Mr. Potts had quit drinking for health reasons but did not mind if guests occasionally had a nip or two. But no drunks or rowdy behavior was allowed. Guests had to have a job or be officially retired. He did not allow able-bodied men who would not work to participate in any way whatsoever.

The conversations were always lively and the stories often had a little spice, but cussing or any other kind of vulgarity was not allowed, especially in the presence of his wife.

None of the men intentionally broke the rules. Most

remembered when Mr. Potts ran a soup kitchen for the homeless during the Depression. Others were children when he established a Boy Scout troop, and a few knew he had been a trustee at the church, for which he still repaired furniture. Some lived in houses that he built, and a couple of them were his tenants. Each was well aware of the fact that Ernest Monroe Potts loved to laugh and tell a good story, but he did not suffer genuine fools lightly.

One afternoon, a short, slender, light-complexioned black man entered Mr. Potts' tool shed and sat down on an empty stool among the regulars.

Mr. Potts stood up, puffed up like a rooster and said, "Look here, mister, I don't allow any old stranger off the street in here. Who are you?"

The stranger grinned and stuck out his right hand. "Ernie, you don't remember me? I'm your old buddy from way back when. I'm John Carr!"

Everybody laughed as the two men embraced each other and Lucius Rouse said, "I remember you from when we were students at the Avery Institute."

"Yeah, that's right," Mr. Potts said. "Both of you went to Avery school in downtown Charleston with all them other children of the rich colored folks. And I remember Mr. John Carr here could swap stories and tell lies with the best of them."

"What was it like going to Avery with all those well-to-do Negroes?" King White asked John Carr.

"Well, not all of us were rich. If you didn't have the money, you had to get a scholarship or work your way through or both. I was good at spelling, and one day the principal, Mr. Benjamin Cox, conducted a spelling contest. I looked forward to it because the winner, if he were a boy, would get a brand new pair of long pants. I didn't have no long pants back then. Wearing long pants was important — made you a man!"

Everyone listened carefully and not one made a sound. John Carr continued. "The day of the spelling bee came and I thought I was ready until I got my first word, which was 'cheese.' So I took a deep breath and closed my eyes so I could see the word in my mind's eye, and said, 'c-h-e-e-s.'

"Well, when I got home that night, I asked Mama for some macaroni and cheese with my dinner, and she shook her head and said, 'If you can't spell it, you can't eat it!'"

The men roared with laughter as Mr. Carr added, "I didn't get the long pants and no young gal in Charleston would be seen with me. So I had to go out with those gals from the country instead!"

Mr. Potts stood up straight and motioned to everyone to settle down. "Now hold on there, Mr. John Carr, I can't have you coming in my place telling better stories than me!"

"What you going to do about it, Ernest?" Hamp Fludd asked.

"Fellows, I'm taking it way back to slavery time. I'm going to tell you about the biggest, baddest smartest slave of them all — Old John!"

"He's got you now!" tall and lanky Hardy Sanders turned and said to Mr. Carr.

And Mr. Potts began:

"Back in slavery times, Old John was so smart that the master never put a whip on his back — not once — according to my granddaddy, and he was there. The master walked up to Old John one day when he was out picking cotton in the fields and struck up a conversation.

"The master, who was wearing his top hat and Sunday suit, said, 'Hey John, how do I look?'

"'Well boss, you looks as mighty as a lion!'

"'That's nice, John, but where did you see a lion? We don't have no lions 'round here.'

"'It was down by the creek kicking up his heels, hollering this and hollering that at the top of his lungs.'

"'John, that was no lion, that was a jackass!'

"'Well sir,' Old John said as he scratched the top of his head. 'You look just like him!'"

John Carr joined the other men laughing and cheering hysterically, and as soon as he regained his composure, he began another story:

"Over in Charleston was this fellow who was as poor as a church mouse, but even so he would not work — not even a job in a pie factory. Somebody told him to go out and dance in the streets and folks would fill up his tin cup and then some, and soon he'd be rich.

"'Ummm,' the fellow said as he thought about the possibilities, and soon thereafter, he strolled over to King Street where the Lincoln Theater and Uncle Sam's Army Surplus Store used to be. As soon as the traffic was clear, he strutted into the middle of the street and started dancing. He crooked his arms down at his elbows and waved them wildly, and he lifted his knees as high as he could and he stomped his feet like a drum major in a marching band, and soon a crowd had gathered around to see what was the matter.

"Then a rich man wearing with a black top hat and a Prince Albert coat walked up and asked, 'Hey you out there in the middle of the street, you want a job?'

"'Sure Mister, you want me to dance in a show?'

"'No, I need an exterminator. My house is full of cockroaches and I like the way you stomp!'"

A thunderous roar of approval shook the walls of the tool shed at that, so much so the steering wheel from Mr. Potts' old '57 Chevy fell from its hook on the wall and hit the floor with a thud.

Mr. Potts frowned a little then reared back and said, "Gimmie room, fellows, I don't know if y'all can handle this one: Old John's master bet his neighbor the whole plantation that John could beat the other master's slave in a fist fight. Later, when Old John's master told him about the bet, John said, 'I'll do it boss. But you'll have to set me free if I win!'

"'Now, John,' his master said, 'I could whip you for saying that!'

"'Old John said, 'Look, if I win, you get to keep this plantation and get the other — What you got to lose except me?'

"The master thought about it for a moment or two, then agreed to proceed with the bet."

All of the men in the shed listened eagerly as Mr. Potts continued: "So on the day of the big fight everybody from all around — white folks and black —gathered in a field to witness the match. Old John warmed up by punching in the air, and the master and his wife looked satisfied. But the other slave had yet to arrive.

"The master went over to Old John and said with a broad smile, 'I guess the other fellow ain't showing up.'

"Then the sky got real dark and the ground began to shake and — boom, boom, boom — something big was about to happen."

Mr. Potts stamped on the floor of the tool shed for emphasis as his audience sat spellbound. Then he continued: "Well, everybody in the field looked up at the same time and saw a slave so big that his shadow blacked out the sky almost completely. And every time that big, black giant put his foot down, the earth shook for miles around.

"Needless to say, Old John's master was real nervous. That's when Old John sauntered over to the master's wife and slapped her across her face — WHAP!

"When the giant saw that, he stopped dead in his tracks, spun around and ran away crying like a girl.

"But the master was not happy. He pulled out his pistol and said, 'John, you got five seconds to tell me why you slapped my wife.'

"Old John smiled real bright and explained, 'We won! I knew if that fellow thought I was bad enough to slap the master's wife, no telling what I'd do to him!'"

The tool shed exploded with laughter, the men stomping their feet and slapping their knees. They cackled so loudly that Mrs. Potts heard them from the kitchen and thought to herself, *Lord have mercy, a pack of wild hyenas has taken over the shed!*

John Carr slowly walked over to Ernest and saluted his old friend, who shook his hand.

"It's getting late, fellas. Time to close up shop," Mr. Potts said.

After everybody went home, Mr. Potts walked up the steps into the kitchen and Mrs. Potts greeted him with a big kiss right on his lips. "Hey Ernie, remember how we used to go out dancing during the war?"

"Yeah," smiled the old man. "Back when I was stationed at Camp Croft in Spartanburg, we'd go to Club Manna and the Swing Club and burn up the dance floor!"

Mrs. Potts smiled, "We should do that again — you know, burn up the floor. Fix the old record player. Please?"

"Use the radio," the old man said.

"There's nothing on this time of day 'cept that music the young folks like. I'm too old for that noise."

"Tell you what," Mr. Potts said, "I'll fix it after we have a snack." Then he headed toward the bathroom. As he crossed through the living room, he glanced out front through the big picture window and saw Lucas on his way to their house from school.

"Lord have mercy," Mr. Potts hollered to his wife, "here he comes."

"Here who comes?"

"Lucas Moore, that's who."

"Now Ernie, you promised to keep an eye on him after school until Amelia gets here."

"I know, but a man gets used to having a little time to himself after working hard all day."

"Yeah, right," she said.

Mr. Potts turned around and glared. It was clear to Mrs. Potts that she should try another approach.

"Look here, I'm a respectable man. I worked hard all my life and still work to keep this place up. Those guys who stop by here are…uh…my customers. I fix all sorts of things for them. Besides, there's nothing wrong with a fellow having some good clean fun with his friends when he leads a busy life!"

"OK, Ernie. And you're a man of your word, too. A promise is a promise."

"All right," Mr. Potts said, "I'll let the boy in."

He opened the door for Lucas.

"Hello," Lucas said, never taking his eyes off the ground.

Mr. Potts scrutinized the boy's thick eyeglasses, scrawny build, poor posture and meek countenance.

This kid sure needs a lot of work, the old man thought to himself.

"Come on in, Lucas. We've been looking forward to seeing you all day," Mrs. Potts said.

Lucas crossed the threshold and entered the house, stopping just inside the doorway. Mr. Potts bent down so that he was eye level with Lucas' huge spectacles.

"Boy, if you're going to spend every day with me, there's

some things you've got to learn. Hold your head up and straighten your shoulders. I can't have you walking around here like that!"

"Yes, sir," Lucas said. He wasn't used to standing up straight at all, much less while walking. He went to the couch and pulled out a book from his bag.

"Lucas, you want something to eat?" Mrs. Potts called as the boy finished reading poetry his teacher had assigned. Lucas was not fond of poetry, but homework assignments were important to him. He got up and went into the dining room where Mr. and Mrs. Potts were seated.

"You may sit there, next to Mr. Potts," Mrs. Potts said. "I've got some buttered biscuits."

Lucas saw freshly baked biscuits in the middle of the table, reached over, grabbed one and gobbled it up before he sat down.

"Hold on there, boy!" the old man said. "I know your mama raised you to do better than that! Now sit down."

Lucas sat, looked over at Mr. Potts and wiped the back of his hand across his mouth, brushing away the crumbs. "Sorry, sir."

"Boy, let me tell you something about being greedy like that. I used to have this uncle named Tillman Brown...."

Mrs. Potts rolled her eyes and sighed. "Not this mess again!"

"Listen carefully now," Mr. Potts continued. "When I was a kid living out in the country, the entire Potts and Brown families came from all over South Carolina for Thanksgiving dinner. Boy, we ate high on the hog. We'd kilt two of our fattest pigs for the occasion. Even with all we ate, there was still plenty of food left over for the trough."

"What's the trough?" Lucas asked.

"That's where you put out leftovers — you know, slop — for the hogs to eat. Anyway, Uncle Till came around with a wheelbarrow full of leftovers and dumped it into the trough. Now, in the hog pen, there was one runt pig way too little to eat. That greedy little pig saw that slop and stars came to his eyes. He just knew he was in heaven. The next morning, Uncle Till went to the hog pen and it was empty."

"Where'd the food go?" Lucas asked.

"Inside that runt, and it killed it dead — his belly was bust wide open from eating too much. Hog guts all over the place, looked like...."

Mrs. Potts obviously had enough of that and scowled at her husband.

"Well, ah," the old man continued, "the point of that story is to always eat like you got some sense."

Mr. Potts glanced sheepishly at his wife, who shook her head saying, "Lord have mercy on my soul."

Mr. Potts pushed back from the table and headed upstairs to start working on the record player. Lucas followed him. As he removed the back of the machine, he noticed Lucas staring at him.

"Don't you have some homework to do?"

"I finished it before our snack."

Mr. Potts rolled his eyes and sighed, "Go watch television then."

"Nothing good on now."

"Fine, you can sit right there. Just don't get in my way."

"I won't."

The old man noticed a loose wire, which he grabbed with his pliers. Lucas craned his neck so he could see. Then he picked up one of the records — an old 78 — and asked, "What kind of music is this? What did you listen to when you were a kid?"

Mr. Potts rolled his eyes and scratched his chin. "We had good music. Not like most of the noise y'all have now. We had folks who could really sing and really play instruments."

"When was that?"

Mr. Potts put the pliers down. "One night years and years ago, I went to County Hall, over in Charleston, to see a show. They had great ones back then. Nowadays, you go to a show and see only one, maybe two performers and it costs way too much money for tickets. Back then, you could see a whole bunch of acts for a dollar."

"Like who?"

"They had this comedian named Stepin Fetchit, for one. I think his real name was Lincoln Perry or something like that," answered the old man. "Step was supposed to be the laziest man on earth, and one night he came on the stage with a wheelbarrow turned upside down.

"Another fellow on stage asked, 'Step, why is that wheelbarrow upside down?'

"Step answered in his lazy voice, 'If I had it right-side up, somebody might put something in it!'"

Mr. Potts laughed and slapped his knees. Lucas just stared.

"Well you see," Mr. Potts explained, "Stepin Fetchit was supposed to be lazy, and if somebody put something in the wheelbarrow, he'd have to work to carry it, and… oh never mind that. But at that same show, a fellow came out on stage and swore he was hot stuff. He had this big guitar and began playing it, but he was just banging on it actually." Mr. Potts stood up and imitated the man playing the instrument to make his point. "That fellow started making all this noise that went *chang iddle lang a chang a chang chang chick a chang iddle langa chang a chang chang* so loud that all you could see was his lips going up and down like he was trying to sing. Who could hear him with all that *chang iddle lang* going on that guitar?"

Lucas laughed.

"But back to the good music," the old man continued. "My favorite song was a little thing by Nat King Cole called 'Straighten Up and Fly Right.' It was a funny little tune about a buzzard flying this monkey somewhere. But while the monkey was on that buzzard's back, he started flying real crazy, going up and down and all around and the poor monkey was hanging on for dear life. See, he planned to drop the monkey and have him for dinner. But that monkey was smart! He grabbed that buzzard by the neck and told him to 'Straighten up and fly right!'"

Lucas' eyes grew wide as he pictured everything Mr. Potts described while the old man mimicked the buzzard. Lucas imagined the monkey holding onto the conniving buzzard in terror.

This led to another round of laughter.

When they calmed down, Mr. Potts went back to work on the phonograph. As he did so, he asked Lucas to hand him various tools. Soon, Amelia arrived to take him home. As they were about to leave Lucas stopped and told her he needed to ask Mr. Potts a question. "Go ahead," she replied, "but I'm tired and need some rest, so don't take long."

Lucas walked over to the old man and asked, "Mr. Potts, do you have any more?"

"Any more what?"

"Stories like that. They're better than anything on television."

Mrs. Potts chuckled and her husband was clearly flattered. "Yeah, I got a million of 'em from just being around for so long. But right now I got to finish with this record player and you got to go home, so I'll tell you more later. And don't forget to straighten up those shoulders!"

Not long after Lucas and his mother left, Mr. Potts finished fixing the phonograph. He placed one of his favorite songs on the turntable and said, "Well, I know I can't swing you around and jitterbug like we used to, but I guess I can still shake a little leg on the floor." He swooped his wife into his arms and led her around the room.

"You know what, Ernie?" Mrs. Potts said.

"What's that?"

"This record player is good for more than just music."

"What are you talking about?"

Mrs. Potts smiled as they continued to dance. "This old

record player fooled somebody else into listening to your old rabbit stories."

Mr. Potts stopped, playfully scowled at his wife and asked, "You want to dance on this floor all by yourself?"

She smiled. He smiled. They resumed dancing as the record played on.

Gators in the Swamp

The next day Mr. Potts was back in the tool shed swapping stories with his friends.

"Yeah," he said, "back during the war when I was stationed at Camp Croft, I was downtown inside a little corner store at Broad and Church streets. This colored lady came in with her two nieces, who looked to be around 10 years old. Well, she asked the white lady who ran the place if her younger niece could use the bathroom. The times being what they was, the white lady said no, so the black lady started to pull the little girl's dress up.

"'Gal, what do you think you're doing?' the store manager asked.

"'If she can't use the bathroom like I asked, she'll do it right out here!' the colored lady responded."

Mr. Potts paused and lit his pipe. "Needless to say, she let the little girl use the bathroom."

After a round of laughter, King White added, "That sounds something like a story that comedian Moms Mabley used to tell."

"Moms was something else," Hamp Fludd said. "Not a tooth in her mouth. Moms said that one time she was driving in Columbia, S.C. and a policeman stopped her and said, 'Girl, I'm gonna write you a ticket.'

"'For what?' she asked.

"'You went through a red light!'

"Moms said, 'I saw y'all white folks going through the green light, so I thought the red one was for us!'"

The men howled with laughter.

"Say what y'all will about Flip Wilson, Bill Cosby, Redd Foxx and all the rest of them comedians, but the grand-daddy of all of them was the great Bert Williams from the West Indies," Mr. Potts said.

"Who?" asked Skeeter Davis, one of the younger men in the shed that day.

"Egbert Austin Williams," Mr. Potts said, exasperated. "I swear y'all young fellows need to read some of these books I've got here on these shelves and learn something. Bert Williams was king of laughs when I was a boy. He came to America when he was a kid and was the first black comedian to make records and movies. He performed for Queen Victoria of England herself! He had one my daddy called 'Oh Death Where Is Thy Sting?' It went a little something like this: An old leather-lunged preacher was up in the pulpit one Sunday banging on the table and whooping and hollering about hellfire and brimstone. 'Weeell,' he said, 'way down in the pits of hell are rivers of moonshine liquor and wild women and juke joints as far as the eye can see, and mountains made of dice and cards. Oh, that hell is a wicked and eee-vil place! Nothing but sin as far as the eye can see! Hell so wicked the Good

Lord himself wouldn't touch it with rubber gloves and a jug of ammonia.'

"This little fellow in the congregation was listening to all this with his eyes wide open and said, 'Pastor, is that true? Is hell filled with wild women and whiskey?'

"The preacher said that it was, and the fellow said, 'Well if what you say is the positive truth, oh death where is thy sting?'"

As the laughter from this story died down, there was a knock at the tool shed door.

"Who is it?" Mr. Potts asked.

"Lucas."

The men placed their cans and bottles behind their chairs as Mr. Potts opened the door and said, "Now look here boy, this is where grown folks are talking. Go on in the house and Lucinda will fix you something to eat."

"Yes, sir."

As Lucas walked toward the house, Mr. Potts stopped and thought for a moment. "Fellows, you know those stories we were talking about earlier with the colored girl not being able to use the bathroom and all?"

"What about them?" Hamp Fludd said.

"That boy and all these little children around here are going to be the first generation of black children to grow up and never know what segregation was like."

The men looked at each other and King White replied, "We hope."

The gathering broke up soon afterward and Mr. Potts headed to the house. After washing his hands, he walked into the kitchen and reached in the cabinet for a box of his beloved graham crackers. He stuck his hand down inside and found only crumbs.

The old man went into the living room where Mrs. Potts and Lucas were sitting on the sofa watching television. Mr. Potts signaled for the boy to follow him. Lucas got up and shuffled nervously behind Mr. Potts back into the kitchen.

Mr. Potts held up the empty box and asked, "Now Luke, how did this happen?"

Luke fidgeted, cleared his throat and replied, "A wild beast ate 'em."

"A what?"

"A wild beast," explained Lucas. "While you were in the shed, a circus parade came by and a wild best was in this cage, see. Anyway, the beast smashed the bars open and headed for the house. He was just about to smash down the front door and eat Mrs. Potts!

"So I ran into the kitchen, grabbed the box of graham crackers and said, 'Here, Mr. Beast! Don't eat Mrs. Potts, please eat these instead!' And guess what, that beast left Mrs. Potts alone and the circus ringmaster came in and gave me a thousand dollars for stopping it."

The old man stared at Lucas for a moment, looked at his wife and said, "OK boy, how does all that explain those graham cracker crumbs around your mouth?"

"Ah, uh…well…." Lucas stuttered.

"Boy, there's one thing you gotta learn. Never try tall tales on an old tall tale-teller like myself! I tried that same mess when I was a kid," Mr. Potts said as Lucas leaned closer to hear what was coming.

"One time my mama cooked a pot of steamed chicken for old Sister Susie Mae, who lived by the swamp not far away. Miss Susie Mae was sickly, so Mama occasionally cooked for her. That day she said to me, 'Ernest, you take this chicken to Sister Susie Mae without fail, you hear?'

"I said, 'Yes, Mama,' and walked off with the pot of steamed chicken. But as I was going down the road, that chicken smelled so good that my belly started growling, and soon thereafter I was sitting on a log and taking the last bite. I thought I was slick. I wiped all the chicken grease off my mouth, went back to the house and told Mama that I was walking by Sister Susie Mae's house down by the swamp...."

"They had swamps around here?" Lucas asked.

"Yeah," Mr. Potts said. "They were where the Jenkins Projects are nowadays. Anyway, I told Mama I would have delivered the chicken if a big gator hadn't crawled up out of the muck and opened his big mouth. I told her that I threw the chicken at that gator so he wouldn't eat me and ran home as fast as I could. There were lots of gators in the swamps back then, so I guess she believed me. She fixed up another pot and told me to deliver it without fail!

"So, as I was passing the swamp on the way to Sister Susie Mae's house, I saw something big moving around in that muddy water. Then some beady eyes poked up, and then come this big mouth, looking like a trap door, and there it was — a giant alligator!"

Lucas was captivated.

"So when that gator rose up from that swamp, I dropped the chicken and ran all the way back home.

"'Boy, what happened to that chicken?' my mama asked.

"I told her the truth and she said, 'Fool me once, shame on you. Fool me twice, shame on me!'

"Then she grabbed a switch from a gum tree in the yard and whipped my behind — bam, bam, bam!"

Lucas laughed as Mr. Potts hopped around, pretending his mother was spanking him. "So remember, boy, watch out when you mess up and lie about it because it'll come back and bite you in the you-know-what."

Lucas went into the next room to do his homework and Mrs. Potts looked at her husband, shook her head and said, "Ernie, you are too much."

"Why you say that?"

"You telling somebody not to tell lies is like a horse telling another horse not to eat oats."

The Letter (and Other Matters)

Lucas Moore often arrived at school feeling sick to his stomach. He was good at his studies and loved to read, but he communicated better with adults than his peers, who teased him mercilessly.

One afternoon after recess, Lucas walked into his classroom and found an envelope on his desk. It had no name, no return address. As his teacher began the lesson, Lucas wondered what was in the letter and who left it for him. As soon as the class was dismissed, Lucas tore open the envelope and read:

Dear Lucas,

I love you. You are so FINE and nice looking that I want to be your girlfriend NOW, and marry you when we grow up. I'll meet you after school today next to the lamppost by the playground at Alhambra Hall Park to talk to you some more.

Love,
Your Secret Admirer

Lucas eagerly waited for school to let out, and when the

bell rang he headed straight to Alhambra Hall Park, five blocks away. He sat on a bench next to the lamppost and didn't wait long before someone with a high-pitched voice behind him said, "Ooooooooh, Lu-cas!"

"Yes?" he said and turned.

That's when Gunther Yates jumped from behind some shrubbery, pointed at Lucas and laughed. "Hey Luke, you wanna know who really wrote that letter?"

Lucas didn't know what to think, and several of his classmates came out from the bushes and laughed as they gathered around him. He took off running.

Then one of the girls turned to Gunther and said, "Boy, please! What you talking 'bout? You didn't write that letter. You couldn't spell 'bee' if one stung you on your behind!"

"Well, I'm the one who thought of it!" Gunther said.

• • •

Lucas was out of breath when he arrived at the Potts' house. He tried to compose himself as he knocked on the front door, and soon Mr. and Mrs. Potts greeted him with broad smiles.

"Hey Luke," Mr. Potts said.

"What's going on?" Luke asked.

"Go look upstairs," Mrs. Potts said. "You won't believe it."

Lucas climbed the steps slowly and heard music — mid-tempo rhythm and blues — coming from one of the bedrooms. Moments later Lucas peeked through the crack in the door and saw a girl — a lovely teenaged girl — with her back to him dancing to music on the radio, performing to a full-length mirror on the wall. She held a brush in one hand, pretending it was a microphone.

When the song ended, she spotted him in the mirror and turned around and shouted, "Luke!"

Valerie Mathewson, Mr. and Mrs. Potts' granddaughter, ran over to Lucas and threw her arms around him. He had not seen Valerie since her family moved away two years ago. She was Lucas' babysitter and often confessed he was the little brother that she never had.

"What are you doing here?" Lucas asked.

"Dad's job brought us back and I'm so excited. It'll be like old times! I'll be here all the time and we'll go to the park and to the movies and to the arcade…just like we used to do, only better!"

Lucas almost cried.

"When did you get the glasses?" she asked.

"Oh, these? Well, not long after you moved." Lucas was very self-conscious about them because they were so big.

"You look smart — like a little professor."

Lucas had heard comments before about his glasses — but they were never compliments.

"Hey, Luke," she said as another tune began. "Let's dance."

She moved gracefully as Luke stumbled over his own feet. But she was patient and instructive, and soon he danced with growing confidence. He thought about the time he tried to dance at a birthday party at the community center not long ago, and everybody, it seemed, laughed him off the floor. Lucas stopped dancing with Valerie and looked down at his feet. "I can't...."

Valerie stopped, bent forward and looked through his big glasses and straight into his eyes. "This shy stuff is not going to work. Loosen up, Luke, if you want to hang with me."

That's when Mrs. Potts came in. "Sorry to break up this little party, Val, but Wallace is on the phone for you."

"He knows I'm back in town?" she asked excitedly.

"Like your granddaddy says, 'People in this town have nothing to talk about but each other,'" Mrs. Potts said.

Valerie ran downstairs to the phone. Lucas slowly followed.

He heard her talking to her childhood sweetheart, heard her saying "Oh, Wallace" this and "Oh, Wallace" that, and "Oh, yes, Wallace, I'd love to go to the football game with you Friday night!"

Luke retreated into the kitchen. He could not stand to hear more. Not long afterward, Valerie stood in the door.

"Luke, I have something for you."

Lucas saw that she was holding a box of candy. She had gone back upstairs to the guest room and got it off the nightstand.

"Don't want any candy," he said, again staring at the floor.

He glanced up for a moment as she reached inside the box and pulled out a white plastic ring.

"What's that?" he asked.

"Listen, Luke," Valerie said as she took his right hand and folded his fingers around the ring. "Whatever happens between Wallace and me, or anyone else for that matter, never forget — you are the little brother I never had and always will be. This will never change. You don't have to wear this ring, just keep it close by as a reminder of a promise I'll keep."

Lucas was on the verge of tears as he heard a car pull into the rock driveway. The driver blew the horn.

"It's my mom. Gotta go now," he said.

As Lucas made his way to the door, Mr. Potts said, "Hey boy, I noticed you looked sad earlier. Anything wrong?"

"Not now," Lucas said as he closed the front door behind him.

The Famous Jackass Story

A few children teased Lucas the next day at school about the incident in the park, but not as much as he had feared. Gunther's inability to spell was the main topic of conversation. Everybody thought that was funny. So by Lucas' standards it was a pretty good day. That afternoon, as he walked to Mr. and Mrs. Potts' house, he tried to think of ways to become popular. He rang the doorbell and, without waiting, entered the living room as the old man was lighting his pipe. Mrs. Potts was in the kitchen brewing coffee. The aromas of the pipe and the coffee were comforting. He felt right at home.

"How ya doing, Luke?" Mr. Potts asked.

"Fine," Lucas said as he removed his jacket and sat down in front of the TV and flipped through the channels. An advertisement for $200 designer warm-up jackets for young people caught his eye.

"It's a shame they charge so much for that," Mrs. Potts said as she sat down across the room.

"It's a bigger shame people are fool enough to buy them," Mr. Potts added.

"I want one," Lucas said.

Mr. Potts coughed and smoke came out the wrong end of his pipe. "You might as well forget that. It don't make good sense to spend that kind of money on something a child will outgrow in a week."

"Lots of kids at school wear that brand," Lucas said.

"And their mamas and daddies are going broke dressing them! You ever heard of Aesop's Fables?"

"No, sir."

"They don't teach nothing worthwhile in school no more," Mr. Potts said as he re-lit his pipe. "Aesop was a slave that lived in ancient Greece. He told lots of stories that explained why people do stupid things. 'Aesop's Fables,' that's what they called his stories. Aesop's stories were so good that some folks didn't like him. They didn't want to hear the truth — made them feel guilty. So a bunch of them jumped Aesop and threw him off a cliff. Killed him dead."

"What's this have to do with those jackets?" Lucas asked.

"Listen carefully," Mr. Pots continued. "One of Aesop's most famous stories was about a jackass."

"Ernie!" Mrs. Potts shouted and Lucas snickered.

"Come on, now," the old man said, "both of y'all know I've got better sense than to curse around children. A jackass is a male donkey."

"Alright, Ernie, go ahead with the story," she sighed.

"See, once upon a time in ancient Greece there was this fella who loaded up his jackass with food and other packages for a long trip. He was walking down the road with the jackass carrying all that stuff on its back when a passerby stopped and said, 'Hey, that jackass is too little to carry all that stuff by himself. Carry it yourself.'

"The man with the jackass thought for a second or two and said, 'That's a good idea.' He took the packages off of the animal's back and carried them himself as the donkey followed."

Mr. Potts coughed again from the smoke, which worried Lucas a little. He had come to really like Mr. Potts and he knew that smoking was bad for the old man. His spirits brightened as Mr. Potts continued:

"While that fool lugged all the packages, another man passed them by and said, 'Hey, mister, why are you straining yourself carrying all those packages when you have a perfectly fine jackass walking behind you?'

"'Uh, yeah, you're absolutely right!' the fool said, then strapped all the packages back on the jackass.

"That guy walked a few more miles with his jackass loaded down with packages and another man passed by and said, 'What kind of lazy bum are you? A big, strong man like you should carry all those packages AND that poor jackass.'

"So the idiot picked up the jackass and the packages, and he sweated and strained down the road while the jackass hee-hawed with glee until they got to the next town. The street was lined with people who were waiting to see the man who was carrying the jackass. Everybody in the crowd was clapping their hands and slapping their thighs and laughing so hard they cried as the man and his jackass walked past them.

"And as that fool with the packages and the jackass on his back approached a small wooden bridge that crossed a flowing stream, everybody shouted as loud as they could, 'Cross the bridge! Cross the bridge!'

"'Uh, yeah! Maybe I should do that,' the fella said, and as soon as he set foot on the bridge: crack, down it came with a tremendous splash!

"'Look at those two jackasses in the water!' somebody screamed and everyone roared with laughter."

Lucas and Mrs. Potts laughed loudly too. Then the old man turned to Lucas and said, "That fool did everything the people in the street told him to do without having the good sense to think for himself. It would be just as dumb if you asked your mama to waste her money on clothes with designer names just to please others, and the designer whose name is on those clothes won't care if your mama can't pay the rent. He'll still have his mansion when she is out on the street."

• • •

After Lucas left that afternoon, Mr. and Mrs. Potts stood in their kitchen finishing off the coffee.

"Nice story, Ernie, but you could have used another example."

"What's that, Lucinda?"

"Remember the time you bought that big Cadillac because 'All the other fellows had one?' We got way behind on the mortgage for that."

"Aw, hush up and let me drink my coffee in peace!" the old man replied.

A Lesson in Growing Up

Lucas walked into Miss Gertrude Doggett's math class seconds before the tardy bell rang. Miss Doggett was prim and proper and seldom smiled. Lucas' mother spoke highly of her, although he wasn't sure why.

"Hello, Lucas. How are you doing?" Miss Doggett asked.

"Fine," Lucas said as he headed for his desk on the front row. But when Natasha Washington walked in and sat beside him, Miss Doggett just scowled.

About halfway through class, Lucas raised his hand and asked to be excused to the bathroom. Upon his return Miss Doggett was standing in front of her students and pointing her finger at Natasha.

"I know you took my pocketbook! You grabbed it when I was writing on the chalkboard."

"I did not take your pocketbook," Natasha said.

"You're a liar with no manners, just like your mother," Miss Doggett said.

Most of the children in the classroom laughed at that, but Natasha started crying.

"Excuse me, Miss Doggett," Lucas raised his hand and said.

"Yes, Lucas, what is it?"

"I think your pocketbook is under your desk."

The children laughed even harder as Natasha folded her arms, Miss Doggett grimaced and the bell rang.

"Thank you, Lucas. Class, dismissed."

Lucas walked with Natasha on the way home. He made her laugh with his imitation of Miss Doggett. When they got to her house, Natasha said, "Sorry Luke, but you can't come into the yard."

"Why?"

"Mama and daddy said never to bring boys even near the house when they aren't home."

"Uh, OK," Lucas shrugged and walked off.

Lucas went straight home because his mother had the day off. Upon his arrival, Amelia Moore greeted her son at the door.

"Mama, may I ask you something about Miss Doggett?"

"Why sure, son. She was my favorite teacher when I was in school."

"But…." Lucas started to say.

"Your grandmother and Miss Doggett were classmates — close friends — way back when they were young. She was nice to me when I was in school and she's very active in the church. What do you want to know about her?"

"Uh, well, nothing really. Is Mr. Potts home?"

"In the shed as usual."

"I'll give him a hand."

"Son, you are blessed to have people like Mr. Potts and Miss Doggett in your life. They set good examples for you," Amelia said.

Lucas found Mr. Potts out back fixing a wheelbarrow. "Hey, Luke, remember when I used to wheel you around in this thing?"

"Yeah," Luke sighed.

"What's the matter, boy?"

Lucas told Mr. Potts what happened at school.

Mr. Potts put his tools away and told Lucas he handled the situation just right.

"Why was Miss Doggett so mean to Natasha?" Lucas asked.

The old man rubbed his chin and said, "Well, Miss Doggett was, uh, shall we say, fond of Natasha's grandfather back when they were young. But he wasn't interested in her. He was interested in Natasha's grandmother. So now, whenever Miss Doggett sees Natasha or her mother, it brings back a lot of bad memories. Maybe if she had gotten married it would be different."

"But Mr. Potts, Natasha and her mama didn't have anything to do with that."

"I know, but some folks don't know how to let things go. They remain bitter all their lives. Now I'm not telling you this to make you think badly of Miss Doggett; I'm just answering your question."

"It shouldn't be like that," Lucas replied.

The old man smiled. "You're growing up, Luke."

"Why do you say that?"

"Well, part of growing up is knowing that 'what should be' and 'what is' are two different things."

Jackie and Joe

The next afternoon Mr. Potts noticed that Lucas had something on his mind. "Still upset over what happened with that Washington girl?" the old man asked.

Lucas nodded.

Mr. Potts filled his pipe with tobacco and struck a match. "After you live awhile, you'll learn how to read people, tell what most of them are thinking by the way they act. Reminds me of Jackie and Joe."

"Who were they?"

The old man blew a cloud of smoke. "Two guys who made the whole world pay attention when they got mad."

"What do you mean?"

"Well Joe grew up in Alabama where things were rough. His entire family had to pick cotton to survive."

"Were they slaves?"

"Not really, but not far from it. They were 'sharecroppers.' They farmed on somebody else's land in exchange for a portion of what was sold. The problem with that was there was nothing left after the boss man took out what he said was the cost of their food and rent. Sharecroppers typically had little education and remained poor all their lives unless they moved up North where they could get jobs in big cities.

"Joe's family moved to Detroit and did OK, but when his parents made him take violin lessons his classmates laughed at him — called him a sissy. So he talked his folks into letting him take boxing lessons."

"Was he any good?" Lucas asked.

"He was really good, so good that he became the heavy-weight champion of the United States. But something happened."

"What?"

Just then, Mrs. Potts walked in with laundry that had been drying on the clothesline.

Mr. Potts continued. "What happened was the United States was about to go to war with Germany. You ever heard of Adolf Hitler?"

"Yeah," Luke said. "He tried to kill all the Jews."

"That's right, along with anybody else he thought was different. He kept saying Germans were better than every-one else. Anyway, it was just before World War II began and Hitler was very proud of a boxer named Max Schmel-ing, the best heavyweight fighter in Germany. Hitler just knew Max could whip Joe, especially since Joe was a black man.

"So in 1936, Joe Louis fought Max Schmeling for the heavyweight championship of the world. It was a tremen-dous bout and Joe lost in the 12th round. The black people in America were sad over that especially since Hitler was running around saying the fight proved that black people were weaker that white people."

"So what happened to Joe?" Luke asked.

"Well, all that bragging and belittling by Hitler made Joe very mad. But Joe didn't waste time moping around saying 'oh poor, poor me' like some people do. He took lemons and made some lemonade. He used his anger to help him to train harder and harder to become the very best fighter in world. And eventually he was back in the ring again with Max Schmeling — only this time in New York City.

"Let me tell you, that was really something. Everybody gathered around radios to hear the fight because they didn't have television back then. So there they were in the middle of Yankee Stadium and we all was praying that Joe would win. We listened to the announcer introduce the fighters, the bell rang and bam!"

"What happened?" Lucas asked.

"Joe took all that anger that had built up inside him over what Hitler said about him and black people into that fight." Mr. Potts swung his arms around like he was in a big fight. "He whopped Schmeling so bad that in two minutes, he was out cold!

"It was like a Negro holiday after that. Black folks all across America danced in the streets because those were rough times for us, and like I said earlier, Joe Louis was the only champ we had in those days. And a funny thing happened after that," Mr. Potts said.

"What?" Lucas asked.

"Joe and Max became really good friends."

The old man paused and sighed. "Yeah, I remember all that like it was yesterday. You know, the only days that really compare to it were when I came back from the war, the day I got married and the day our daughter was born. That's how important Joe was to us back then. He still is in a way."

Mrs. Potts, who was folding the clothes and listening, smiled.

"So who was Jackie?" Lucas asked.

"Jackie was a baseball player. When I was stationed at Camp Croft in Spartanburg during the war, I saw him play at Duncan Park in the Negro leagues. Jackie Robinson played with Satchel Paige for the Kansas City Monarchs. They were taking on the Spartanburg Sluggers."

"What kind of leagues?"

"The Negro leagues. The old black baseball teams before they let black folks play in the majors."

"When did blacks start playing for the majors?"

"Well, that's where Jackie comes in. He was a smart fellow who went to college, served in the Army and played in the Negro leagues. There was a white man named Branch Rickey who owned the Brooklyn Dodgers, which was a major league team that later moved to Los Angeles. Rickey decided it was time to have a black player. But he couldn't have just any black player. He wanted one smart enough to understand that if he fought back against real prejudiced people, it would cause a riot.

"So Jackie tried out for Rickey's Montreal team up in Canada in 1946. Jackie did really well up there, and in

1947, he was brought down to Brooklyn, and that was dangerous."

"Why?"

"A lot of white people hated black folks in those days, for reasons I'll explain later. At first, some of Jackie's own teammates in Brooklyn didn't want to play with him. But Branch Rickey threatened to throw them off the team if they didn't straighten up. Jackie soon proved himself to be an excellent player and a respected teammate. When he played, other teams treated Jackie so badly that his teammates said, 'That's enough!' They saw that Jackie was a smart and good man, so they stuck up for him."

Mr. Potts sighed. "The people who didn't know Jackie sure gave him a rough way to go. One time somebody threw a black cat on the field and yelled, 'Look Jackie, here's your cousin.' Of course Jackie didn't like it. But he put all that anger into being such a good player that he made Rookie of the Year in 1947. That meant a lot in those days."

"So what does this have to do with me?" Lucas asked.

"Plenty. If Jackie and Joe let all of that misery get to them, nobody today would have given a hoot about them. But they put the energy they could have wasted being angry into being the best they could be. You're going to see a lot of things in life that will make you mad, but don't just sit there and mope. Get up off your behind and do something about it. Put all your energy into being the best you can be. Then maybe one day somebody will tell their kids about Lucas Moore like I'm telling you now about

Jackie Robinson and Joe Louis."

Lucas moved to the kitchen table to finish his home-work. Mr. Potts went outside to work on a lawn mower, and Mrs. Potts followed. The mower wouldn't start so the old man shouted and kicked the engine.

"Now, Ernie," Mrs. Potts said. "Practice what you preach!"

The Devil and His Wife

During an unusually rainy afternoon, Mr. Ernest Potts looked out of the window and then at his watch.

"What you waiting for, Ernie?" Mrs. Potts asked as she shelled pecans at the kitchen table.

"Oh," sighed the old man as he adjusted his glasses and walked over to her. "It's about time for Luke to get here from school."

Mrs. Potts chuckled. "At first you didn't want to be bothered with that boy coming here every day. Now you can't wait 'til he does."

"No, it ain't that. It's just that, well, I don't want the little fellow to catch cold from being out in all this rain. Besides...."

The front doorbell rang and Mrs. Potts hurried over to open it. Lucas stood on the doorstep with his raincoat over his head and his books in his arms. He stepped into the hall and Mrs. Potts helped remove his rain-soaked jacket while the old man turned up the heat.

"You OK, Luke?" she asked.

"Yes, ma'am," he replied.

"Go stand in front of the heater over there and you'll

be fine in just a few minutes."

Lucas worked on his homework as the rain came down. About an hour later Mr. Potts went back to the window. "Hey, Luke, come here. You've got to see this!"

Mr. Potts held Lucas' shoulder as he pointed out of the picture window. Lucas looked and his eyes widened. "It's raining and the sun is shining at the same time!"

"Yep," smiled Mr. Potts as he pulled on his suspenders. "The devil's beating his wife."

"For REAL?"

The old man chuckled and relit his pipe. "That's what some say when we get the sun and the rain at the same time."

Before this discussion could continue, the doorbell rang again and Mrs. Potts left the kitchen to answer the door. It was Lucas' mother.

"Hello, cute self," Mr. Potts said as she entered the room.

"How y'all doing?" Amelia asked. "Where's Luke?"

"Oh," answered Mr. Potts, "he's right over...wait a minute! I was talking to him a second ago."

"You think he went outside?" Mrs. Potts asked.

"I hope not. It's still raining," Amelia replied.

"Really?" Mrs. Potts said. "I could have sworn I saw the sun shining just now and...hey, look outside!"

The ladies looked out of the picture window and saw Lucas with one of Mr. Potts' shovels digging in the ground in the middle of the sun shower. They hurried outside, grabbed the boy by the arm and ran back into the house.

"What were you doing digging outside in the rain?"

his mother asked.

"I just wanted to see the big fight."

"What big fight?" Mrs. Potts asked.

"Mr. Potts said that whenever the sun is shining and it's raining, the devil is beating his wife."

Mrs. Potts groaned as she shook her head. "I ain't heard that old fool mess since I was a little girl."

The ladies looked at each other for a moment, then turned to Ernest Potts as he sat in his easy chair with the newspaper up to his face.

"Ernest," Mrs. Potts said.

The old man slowly let the newspaper down, looked at his wife and smiled.

Purple Cows and Green Trees

One Saturday Lucas stopped by to see Mr. Potts. The old man was in the back yard by the tool shed chewing gum instead of smoking his ever-present pipe. A couple of books were open on the ground near the lawn-mower engine that he was fixing.

"What happened to your pipe?" Lucas asked.

"Oh," replied the old man as he chewed his gum, "you know all that coughing I do sometimes? The doctor said I have to give up the pipe if I want to stay around for awhile. Besides, smoking that pipe around you wasn't a good idea anyway if I'm gonna set an example. Have a stick?" He offered Lucas a piece of Doublemint gum.

"Sure, thanks. What's with the books on the ground?"

"How do you think I got so smart? No matter how old you are, a day is wasted if you don't learn something new."

"Whoo-eee!" Some one screamed from across the yard. Lucas turned around and saw Frederick Spears, the town drunkard. "Clap your hands and stand up and cheer 'cause Frederick Davidson Spears is here!" the man said as he walked up.

"And here is a prime example of what I'm talking about,"

mumbled Mr. Potts. "What do you want?"

"Hello, Mr. Potts!" Frederick Spears pulled a pint of Mad Dog wine out of his pocket. "Want some?"

Ernest scowled, pointed at Lucas and told the tramp, "Number one, I don't drink that junk. Number two, you need to show some respect. There's a child here!"

"So what? I was drinkin' worse than I do now when I was his age. There's some left for him too if he wants it!"

Mr. Potts sighed, turned to Lucas and said, "Boy, it's a good idea if you take one of these books here, go on the other side of the shed and read it."

Lucas took a book about the baseball player Jackie Robinson. He found it fascinating. It confirmed what Mr. Potts told him earlier about the famed athlete. From his position, he could also hear Frederick Spears cursing loudly at Mr. Potts. To his surprise, the old man remained silent. After a few minutes of the drunk's tirade, Mr. Potts said, "Alright Freddie, you finished yet?"

"Uh, yeah. I ain't got nothing else to say."

"Good," Mr. Potts said. "Now kindly remove yourself from my property."

Frederick staggered off and down the street.

"Lucas, come on back over here and I'll show you how to fix this lawn mower," Mr. Potts said.

Lucas did as he was told, and after assisting Mr. Potts for a few minutes, Lucas asked, "Sir, could I ask you a question?"

"You just did. Ask me another one."

"How come you didn't say anything while Mr. Spears

was talking all that trash?"

Mr. Potts put down his tools, wiped his hands and explained. "For a very good reason. I'll put it to you like this: I once knew this fellow who thought he was the smartest guy in town. He was walking down the street one day, just as happy as he could be, when all of a sudden some other joker walked up to him and said, 'Hey, you know what? Purple cows fall from green trees!'"

Lucas laughed as Mr. Potts proceeded, "Now the fellow who thought he was real smart replied like he was the King of England, 'You sir, are a rather stupid man! Purple cows do not fall out of any green trees!'

"'Ya lie!' said the fool. 'Purple cows do fall from green trees.'

"'You are most certainly an ignoramus!' the smart one said. 'I assure you that purple cows do not fall from any green trees.'

"So sure enough, a group of people started to gather around to see what the argument was about. And you know what the people said?"

"What?"

The old man smiled again, "The people said, 'Look at them two fools.'"

Lucas wasn't sure what to make of that.

Then Mr. Potts asked, "Do you consider Frederick Spears to be a wise man?"

"No."

"Do you consider me to be a fool?"

"No, sir."

"Very good. That's why I didn't argue with Mr. Spears. Wise men don't argue with fools. They pay no attention to fools and go on about their business."

Lucas smiled as his mother turned into the driveway. "Thank you for letting me read your book about Jackie Robinson."

"You can keep it. I'd rather see you fill your mind with that rather than what Mr. Spears pollutes his body with."

Lucas left and the old man adjusted the lawn mower. He pulled the starter rope and the engine clicked and sputtered then went dead. He threw his cap on the ground and shouted, "Hot dang! Bunch of junk!" He was about to kick the lawn mower when he looked up and saw Lucas getting into the car with the book in his hand.

"Well, at least I did one thing right today," he smiled and said.

My Hero

Lucas was jumping up and down as he came through the door.

"What's the matter?" Mr. Potts asked.

"Frankie Charles is going to be at the community center today!"

Mrs. Potts, who was knitting nearby, stuck herself in her finger.

"Frankie Charles?" Mr. Potts was almost as excited as Lucas. "I wouldn't mind seeing him. He scored four touchdowns in the championship game."

"Yes, sir! He's gonna sign autographs!"

"Well what are you waiting for?" Mr. Potts asked. "See if you can get one for me while you're at it!"

Mr. Potts smiled as Lucas darted out of the door. "That boy's as excited about Frankie Charles as I used to be about Jackie Robinson and Joe Louis."

The old man turned to his wife and said, "I guess you wouldn't know nothing about Frankie Charles."

"For your information, Ernest Potts, I know a lot more about Frankie Charles than you do!"

"Oh really? And what, may I ask, do you know about

Frankie Charles?"

"One of my church sisters is Frankie Charles' cousin. I didn't want to say anything in front of the boy, but I have news for you about Mister Franklin Charles."

When Lucas arrived at the community center, he saw a big platform set up outside for Frankie Charles. Hundreds of children waited to see him. Several minutes later, the crowd cheered as a black limousine pulled up and Frankie Charles, wearing a black suit and sunglasses, stepped out and made his way up to the platform.

Lucas looked in awe as Frankie got up to the microphone and said, "Kids, there are three things you gotta do if you want to be like me. You gotta work hard, stay in school and just say no to those drugs!" The children cheered loudly as did the handful of adults in the audience.

Just as Frankie was about to continue his speech, the crowd heard a loud siren then a police cruiser pulled up. Two officers jumped out of the car, drew their guns and said, "Freeze Frankie, you're under arrest!"

Lucas and the rest of the crowd gasped. Frankie was about to run, but another cruiser full of policemen pulled up and surrounded him. Frankie held up his hands and the officers searched his pockets. One yelled, "Got it!" and pulled out a plastic bag filled with what appeared to be some sort of illegal drug.

The children booed and threw rocks at Frankie as the policemen handcuffed the football star, read him his rights and ordered him to get in one of the squad cars. Lucas hung his head and walked slowly and sadly back to the

Potts' residence.

"Well," said Mrs. Potts as she opened the door. "What happened?"

"Frankie Charles got arrested," Lucas said.

She took him into her arms and mumbled, "Frankie's a heroin addict."

"You want another hero?" Mr. Potts asked calmly.

"Who?" Lucas asked.

"Go in the front bedroom. He's waiting for you."

Lucas trudged to the front bedroom and as he opened the door, he noticed something that stood directly in front of him — a mirror.

The Curse

Mrs. Potts rocked contentedly in her rocking chair while working on her needlepoint. Mr. Potts sat nearby in his easy chair reading the front section of the newspaper while Lucas sat on the carpet reading the movie ads and cartoons, which were spread across the floor. The late afternoon sun shone through the picture window setting the room aglow.

Lucas got up to throw away the wrapper from the candy bar he had just finished when Mr. Potts said, "Luke, take out the trash while you're up."

"Where do you want me to take it?"

"Out by the fence in the front yard."

Just as Lucas made it to the front yard, the trash truck arrived. Connie Smalls, one of the local sanitation workers, jumped off the back of the truck, went to the fence and emptied the Potts' container.

Lucas noticed the knot of a necktie peeping out from under Mr. Smalls' overalls. As soon as Lucas got back to the house he asked Mr. Potts why Mr. Smalls was wearing a tie.

"Ever heard of Booker T. Washington?" Mr. Potts asked.

"I read about him in school."

"Did you know that when he was enslaved he left the plantation and walked across two states in order to get an education? Later, when he was grown, he started the Tuskegee School in Alabama. Anyway, Herbert, uh...." Mr. Potts paused for a moment.

Mrs. Potts looked up startled and Lucas asked, "Why'd you call me Herbert?"

"Oh, uh, just a slip of the tongue," Mr. Potts said. "Anyway, Booker T. Washington once made a speech and said that there is as much dignity in tilling a field as there is in writing a poem. Know what that means?"

"No, sir."

"It means that as long as you're doing honest work, you should be proud of what you do. The farmer who tills the field does hot and dirty work, and some people look down on that, but it's important because he helps feed people, just as the poet writes things that help feed people's minds, you see? They're both important. Now as for Connie Smalls, a lot of people look down on what he does because he takes other people's trash, but they look up to people who go to work and wear a tie. So one day he told me that wearing a tie is his way of showing people that his work is important too. Got it?"

"I think so." Lucas excused himself to go to the bathroom.

Mrs. Potts glared at her husband, who said, "Look Lucinda, I'm sorry about that."

"It's all right Ernie. I understand. Besides, you told the boy right about Connie Smalls."

As Lucas returned from the bathroom, Mrs. Potts got up to check on her crescent rolls baking in the oven. Mr. Potts saw something highly amusing in the newspaper and let out one of his loud, open-mouthed guffaws. Lucas looked up and noticed a huge space in the old man's upper row of teeth.

"Mr. Potts, what happened to your tooth?"

Mr. Potts was caught off guard by this question, but he was in a good mood so he answered. "Back when I was a little boy we didn't get water from the faucet like we do now. We had to go outside and pump water up from the well."

Lucas sat listening.

"Anyway, my dad had asked me to go out and pump some water so he could wash up for a church meeting. So I got the pail and went to the pump and primed it and started pumping water." The old man went through the motions of pumping water as he told his story.

"In the middle of that, I heard my daddy call me, so I turned around to see what he wanted. Soon as I let go of that pump, the pressure made that level jump up and hit my mouth — whap! That tooth's been gone ever since. It's important to pay attention to what you're doing!"

As Mr. Potts returned to his newspaper, Lucas looked on the mantle where family photos were displayed and noticed an Army picture of the old man with an open-mouthed smile and a full set of teeth. Lucas chuckled to himself. He understood that sometimes Mr. Potts stretched the truth a little because he loved to entertain people with his tales.

Lucas quietly went into the kitchen where Mrs. Potts was bent over taking the rolls out of the oven.

"Mrs. Potts, may I ask you a question?"

She stood up and said, "Of course, dear. What is it?"

"How did Mr. Potts get that gap in his teeth?"

"Oh. He had to go to the dentist a few years ago and get it pulled because of a real bad cavity. Why do you ask?"

"Just wondered."

"Have some," said Mrs. Potts and offered Lucas a piece of bread.

He thanked her and returned to the living room.

Mrs. Potts walked in and looked out of the picture window. "Look out Ernie, your buddy Mandy Brown is headed this way."

The name "Mandy Brown" sounded very familiar to Lucas.

"Uh uh!" shouted the old man as he jumped up and angrily threw his newspaper to the floor. "I am not having that ignorant cackling hen in my house talking her stupid mess!"

"Ernie!" shouted Mrs. Potts as she pointed to Lucas.

"I don't care! This is my house and I don't need to sit in my own house and listen to all that fool talk!"

He stormed into the kitchen while his wife followed, pleading for him to calm down.

The doorbell rang and Lucas answered the door. He immediately recognized Mandy Brown. She was a janitress at his school who had made it known that she did not like Lucas.

"Hey, Lucinda," bellowed Mandy as she entered the Potts' home. "You know that Emma Lou Mason who act like that daughter of hers is pure like snow? Well, Susie just tell me that fresh little heifer done gone out with the preacher's boy and got herself…."

Mandy stopped, looked around the room and realized that Mrs. Potts was not there. She looked at Lucas with a puzzled expression.

"You is Amelia Moore's boy."

"Yes, ma'am."

"Oh yeah, I heard about your daddy. He drop dead a few months ago."

Lucas turned away and picked up a section of the newspaper.

"You sure does a lot of reading, boy."

"I like to read."

"It ain't good for a little fellow like you to do all that reading. You need to go out and play."

"I ride my bike and play ball. Why do you say it's not good for me to read?"

"Stuffing your brain like that ain't gonna do nothing but make you an educated fool. All you need is to know enough to get a job when you get big. Some things just ain't for us."

"I don't understand what you mean."

"Reading is for white folk! Even the Bible say us colored people was cursed! The white folk do the thinking and colored folks do the working."

Her tirade was suddenly interrupted by the sound of

clapping from the kitchen. Lucas and Mandy turned to see Mr. Potts entering the living room from the kitchen, and he was applauding.

"Amen, hallelujah!" said Mr. Potts as he continued to clap. "That's right on the ball, Mandy! You sure told that boy some good stuff." Everyone, including Mrs. Potts, was puzzled by Ernie's response.

"Uh, thank you," said Mandy, who had never heard Mr. Potts say anything kind to her.

"I am so impressed by your wealth of Biblical knowledge that I want to hear some more!" Mr. Potts reached to his bookshelf and grabbed his Bible, which he held out toward Mandy. "Show us the light, Mandy! Come on and give us some more of that good preaching!"

Mandy was horrified. "Well Ernie, I done left my glasses home and...."

"I figured you'd say that," Mr. Potts said as he reached into a drawer next to the bookshelf and pulled out a magnifying glass. "Here, this ought to do it. Give us a sampling of some good old-time religion."

"Well," Mandy said as her hands shook. "Um, I got to go on home anyhow. My eyes is tired and I ain't feeling too good."

As Mandy headed out the door, Mr. Potts slapped his knees and roared with laughter. Mrs. Potts shook her head and said, "Ernie, I don't know what I'm going to do with you!"

Lucas, rather confused, asked, "Mr. Potts, why couldn't Miss Mandy read the Bible?"

The old man stopped chuckling and explained. "Lucas, she can't even read her own name."

Mrs. Potts scowled and quickly explained. "It's not really all her fault, Lucas. Back in slavery times, our grandparents couldn't go to school. But after slavery, they started building schools for the black folks, and my parents and Ernie's parents saw to it that we went to them."

"But what about Miss Mandy and what she said about the Bible?"

Mr. Potts sighed. "Back in the slavery times, most of the masters understood that they had to keep the slaves ignorant because the smart ones would run away. So they filled their minds with junk like 'Black folks is ignorant by nature,' and 'Colored people are good with anything involving the body but nothing with the mind,' and 'Reading and speaking well is for white people but will drive us crazy,' and 'The Bible said Negroes were cursed as slaves,' and so on. None of that fool mess was true, but if you were kept from reading and going to school you wouldn't know any better.

"Our grandparents who were slaves and our parents knew better. But Mandy's mama kept her in the fields when she should have been at school. Like I said earlier, there's nothing wrong with working in the fields. That's honest work. But if you have a chance to get an education and do better, then do better and don't knock other folks."

Mrs. Potts quickly added, "Lucas, you've got to understand that a lot of people back then couldn't go to school because they had to work to live."

"We were all poor back then," Mr. Potts continued, giving his wife a look. "But there is a difference between being uneducated and being ignorant. Our parents and grandparents were uneducated, but they had enough sense to want something better for us and sent us to school. Mandy's mama couldn't see that. I don't dislike Mandy for being ignorant, but she does and says a lot of mean and hateful things because of her ignorance."

"But slavery stopped a long time ago," Lucas said. "Why does she still think like that?"

The old man thought for a moment, searching for a good explanation. "Remember when your dad was alive and we had that dog named No-Name?"

"Oh yeah," Lucas said. "She had all of those puppies!"

"That's right," answered Mr. Potts with a chuckle. "Valerie couldn't figure out what to call her, so we named her 'No-Name.' That old dog was a mess, wasn't she? Anyway, No-Name had four pups: Sam, Pal, Frisky and Boxer. When you were about 5 years old, your dad took Boxer home as a present for you."

"Yeah, I remember that, and when Boxer got big, Dad put a chain around his neck as a leash for him in the back yard."

"He sure did. Even then, you didn't like to see dogs all chained up, so you asked Robert to build a little fence for the yard so Boxer could run around in it. I came over and helped. And right after we finished, we freed Boxer from that chain and a cat happened to walk by. Boxer started to bark and run after the cat but stopped suddenly and strained and barked some more at the cat. It was as if that chain was still around his neck."

"Yeah, I remember."

Mr. Potts let out a heavy sigh. "See, some folks are like that too. Some of our folks, even when they were slaves, knew that there was something better out there for them. So when slavery was over and the first schools for us opened, they sent us to them so we could do better. But others like Mandy's folks couldn't see that. All they knew was what they saw, so Mandy's grandmama and her mama passed all that ignorance and slave thinking down to her. That's why she's bitter and hates anybody who's doing better than her now, and that's why she tells you that junk. That's how it is with some people. They let themselves get cursed by what happened to their ancestors instead of getting up and doing something better for the future."

"Either way," Mrs. Potts said, "always be nice to people even if they can't read and write. It could have been you if you were in a different family."

Mr. Potts paused, giving his wife a sharp glance. "That's true, but in this day and time, they have night schools for grown people to learn how to read and write. If somebody knocks you down, that's his or her fault. If you stay down, that's your fault."

Lucas' mother arrived just then. After bidding farewell to Lucas and his mother, Mr. Potts went to pick up his Bible again and said to his wife, "You know, Lucinda, I see why they call this the Good Book!"

The old lady laughed. "Ernie, it's good to hear you say that."

"Yes, ma'am. Any book that could help me get that fool Mandy out of my house has to be good!"

"Ernest Potts, you need to stop with that foolishness!" Mrs. Potts grabbed a throw pillow and hit her husband over the head with it. Both of them laughed.

A Day in the Park

The next day at school, Mandy Brown conveniently ignored Lucas, but since he understood the situation, it did not bother him.

The day was uneventful. After the bell rang, Lucas walked with most of the children through Alhambra Hall Park, between the school and his neighborhood. They would often stop to enjoy the playground on the way to their homes.

As the children took their turns on the swings, slides and monkey bars, Lucas noticed Natasha Washington jumping rope with her girlfriends. He waited until she had finished her turn jumping. He recalled the time a few weeks earlier when he comforted her after Miss Doggett insulted her in class. As she chatted with her friends after jumping rope, Lucas walked up to her and said hello.

Suddenly, the other girls began laughing and one asked, "Natasha, you can't do better than that?"

Natasha looked around in shame and said to Luke, "Boy, get from around me. What would I want with somebody weird and ugly like you?"

Luke was caught off guard and did not know how to

respond. He slowly walked away with their laughter ringing in his ears.

A few minutes later, Lucas arrived at the Potts' house and rang the bell. To his relief, Valerie answered the door.

"Hey, buddy. How was school?"

"Not bad, Valerie. Where are Mr. and Mrs. Potts?"

"Granddaddy's at the church talking to the preacher about making some furniture for him. Grandmama went with him since her church sisters were having a meeting too."

"Oh, OK," Lucas sighed.

Just then, the phone rang and Valerie answered, then said, "Hey lover boy, it's for you."

Lucas wondered who would be calling him, especially at the Potts' house. As he held the phone's receiver, he heard Natasha's voice. "Hey Luke, sorry about what happened. I was with my friends and wasn't thinking. But look, if you want to talk sometime maybe...."

Lucas slammed the phone down and said nothing.

Valerie returned to the living room. "Well, well, well. Some little playground lover is giving me competition. Trying to steal my buddy from me, huh?"

Lucas pushed her hand away. "She's not my girlfriend. I don't want to talk about it!"

Valerie quickly changed the subject.

"OK, look, I noticed you don't have any books with you today, so I take it you don't have any homework, right?"

Lucas nodded.

"Good, I don't either. It's a nice day, so let's go to the park."

Lucas hoped that his classmates would be gone by the time they got there. He did not say anything about it though because he did not want to explain the situation to Valerie. So they set off for Alhambra Hall Park.

As they were walking, they passed a group of little white girls who were about Lucas' age playing hopscotch. Lucas strained to see if he recognized any of them from school. He had seen a few of them in some other classes, but as with most of the school's white children, he did not know them very well.

The girls jumped on numbers written on the hopscotch boxes on the sidewalk. Suddenly, a mischievous look appeared on Valerie's face as she shouted, "Give me room and I'll show y'all how it's done!"

Lucas watched as the free-spirited teenager ran over and rapidly skipped over the hopscotch diagram. Val triumphantly placed her hands on her hips and said, "It's been a while, but I've still got it!"

Lucas admired Valerie's boldness. "You're not shy about anything, Val."

"Nahhh, life's too short for that, Luke."

"How did you get to be like that?"

"Let's see, when I was 6 years old, not too long before you were born, grandmama and granddaddy took me shopping downtown on King Street. We were over by Honest John Pembroke's record store when…."

"I remember Honest John," Luke interrupted. "He used to be on the radio when I was little."

"Way back when you were a kid, huh?"

"Yeah, and before that, too," Lucas chuckled.

"Anyway," Valerie continued, "Honest John was playing 'Dancing in the Streets' by Martha Reeves and the Vandellas and I got in the middle of the sidewalk and started doing just that — snapping my fingers and doing the twist. I was so happy and free that the people stopped on the sidewalk to watch."

"'Stop that! That's not ladylike!' Grandmama shouted.

"Then granddaddy said, 'It's OK, this child has plenty of time to be a lady. Long as she's not hurting herself or anybody else, let her enjoy her life while she can.'

"I've been enjoying it ever since," Valerie said.

Soon they stopped to buy hot dogs and sodas from a park vendor, and Lucas saw that his classmates had already gone home. After enjoying their snacks, they walked by the swing sets.

"Remember how I used to push you on this?" Valerie asked. "Well this time I'd like for you to push me."

Valerie got into a swing and Lucas tried to push her. His arms strained and struggled but he could not get Valerie's larger body airborne.

"Hey, what's wrong back there?" she asked.

"I-I can't move you."

Valerie jumped up and looked down at the boy, "What are you trying to say, that I'm too big for you to push? That I'm getting fat? That I'm big like a hog?"

The boy looked horrified, "Oh no, I'd never say anything like that about you, Val!"

"Humph. Next thing you'll be saying is that I have a

butt like a horse! Is that what you're trying to say? That I've got a big butt?"

"No, Valerie! Really, I'd never say that!"

Valerie paused for a moment and knelt down to the boy's eye level. "Hey, look, you really have to lighten up. Stop taking things so seriously. What's gotten into you?"

Luke looked sad.

"I don't know, Val. Since Dad died, it's been rough. I've never been that good at sports — I can't catch, I can't dance and everybody laughs at me for looking strange, especially since I got my glasses."

Valerie thought for a minute. "What do you do when they laugh at you?"

Lucas shook his head but didn't answer.

Valerie put her arm around him and they headed back to the house. "You don't know what to say when they do that, do you?"

Lucas shook his head again.

"Luke, you've gotta stand up to them. Let them know you're no joke. Hold your head up and walk straighter. Now as for that other stuff, what can you do?"

"Huh?"

"You just said what you can't do, so tell me what you can do."

Lucas thought for a moment. "Let's see, I'm good at drawing. I like to read and I like to write stuff."

"Good. Stop worrying about what you're not good at doing and work on what you are good at doing. Maybe one day you'll draw and write so well that people who once gave you a hard time will be proud to say they knew you."

"You think so?"

"That's how most people get started. But remember you have to hold your head up and walk proudly. Look people in the eye. Let them know they're dealing with somebody. If you don't believe in you, nobody else will either."

Lucas appreciated this advice. At least he could talk to Valerie without being embarrassed and he sensed that he could tell her things confidentially. Soon, they arrived at the Potts' home.

Valerie noticed an old baseball on the lawn. She ran over and picked it up. "Hey, Luke!"

As Lucas turned around, Valerie threw the baseball directly toward his head. He caught the ball just before it hit him in the face. Valerie laughed and said, "Thought you said you couldn't catch!"

Luke thought for a moment, and then a huge smile came across his face. He repeatedly tossed the ball into the air and caught it as he walked home.

Just Like the Fox

The next day Miss Doggett began the American history lesson.

"Class, we are going to continue where we left off on our history lesson from yesterday. Now, does anyone remember what Booker T. Washington was famous for?"

Miss Doggett noticed Gunther Yates in the back of the classroom chatting away with his friends so she said sternly, "Gunther, who was Booker T. Washington?"

The boy was caught off guard just as Miss Doggett had expected. "He, ah…was the guy that chopped down the cherry tree, right?"

The class laughed, "Of course not!" Miss Doggett said. "Does anyone know the correct answer?"

Gunther turned beet red. Lucas excitedly raised his hand and said, "I know, he was the guy who was born a slave and went on to run the Tuskegee school down in Alabama."

"That's right!" Miss Doggett said with a smile, "and it's still a very good school. Now class, while he was at Tuskegee.…"

Gunther fumed at Lucas and whispered to his circle of friends at the back of the class.

Several hours later, the school bell rang and the students eagerly walked from the building into the glowing sunshine of the afternoon. A plethora of bicycles and skateboards exited the schoolyard while a large number of students who lived nearby walked home. It was Friday!

Lucas was beginning to walk to Mr. Potts' house, alone as usual, when he had the strange feeling that something was about to happen. He noticed a group of shadows reflected on the ground directly in front of him. He began to pick up his pace when he heard a voice say:

"Hey, smart boy! Going someplace?"

Lucas shut his eyes and nervously turned around. He opened his eyes slowly and saw Gunther Yates and his friends smiling maliciously.

"Luke," Gunther said as he stepped up to Lucas and looked down on him. "You're smart, so here's what we gonna do. I know I ain't as bright as you when it comes to school, so I'm gonna let you hit me as hard as you can."

Lucas began to shake nervously. "For real, Gunther?"

Gunther nodded. "Go ahead."

Lucas shut his eyes and balled his tiny fist as hard as he could until his veins bulged and swung into the larger boy's chest as hard as he could. Thud!

Gunther looked down at his chest, turned to the other boys, and said, "Man, I had mosquitoes bite me harder than that." He turned back to Lucas. "That the best you can do?"

"Yes," Lucas said as he stood there shaking.

"Well, it's my turn now," Gunther said as he balled up

his fist and the other kids started laughing. "Let me show you how hard I can hit!"

Before the smaller boy could collect himself, Gunther landed a right hook on Lucas' chin. Lucas dropped to his knees. Dazed, he looked up and gingerly touched his throbbing jaw. Gunther and the others laughed as they walked away.

As he staggered to get up and regain his balance, Lucas felt weak and ashamed. He headed to the Potts' house. He knew this would be all over school on Monday and everyone would hear about it and laugh at him. Worst of all, he feared his mother would see how he looked and raise such a fuss that she would embarrass him even more.

Lucas entered the Potts' home with his bruised face and tattered shirt. This did not escape the attention of Mr. Potts.

"What's the matter, Luke?" asked the old man as his wife stepped back in surprise.

Lucas sighed. It was clear that he didn't want to talk about this.

"Look," Mr. Potts said. "You can either tell me what's going on, or we can discuss it with your mama, who will go straight to the school and find out what happened."

"That's OK Mr. Potts, I'll tell you."

"Good answer. Now what's going on?"

"Gunther hit me."

The old man grimaced. "That Yates boy! Look here, you either have to leave him alone or stand up to him."

"It wasn't just him," Lucas explained. "It was a bunch of his friends too," and he told Mr. Potts all that happened.

Mr. Potts thought for a moment and said, "It is hard to stand up for yourself if you're outnumbered like that. They were acting like a lynch mob!"

Mrs. Potts added, "I'll call Gunther's mama and see what we can do to put a stop to this mess."

"At least you stood up for yourself, and that's good," Mr. Potts continued. "That Gunther, he's not the sharpest tool in the shed, I'd bet. Is he?"

Lucas thought for a minute and shook his head.

The old man chuckled. "Just as I figured. Remember that story I told you about Aesop?"

"About the jackass, right?"

"Yeah, Mr. Aesop told another one that reminds me of this mess with Gunther. It was about a fox."

Lucas cocked his head to the side. His jaw hurt.

"There was this fox walking through the woods enjoying himself when all of a sudden he felt a hard whack. The fox screamed in pain and when he looked down, he saw that a fox trap had cut off his tail."

"The fox was very unhappy because foxes are very proud of their long fluffy tails, see." Mr. Potts put a stick of gum in his mouth before continuing this tale. "Boy, I sure do miss my pipe," he muttered.

"Huh?" asked Lucas.

"Oh, ah, nothing Luke," said the old man. "Anyway, the fox was walking around crying over losing his tail when he stopped by the lake and saw some other foxes swimming around and admiring their pretty tails. So he was envious, and decided to play a trick on them."

"What did he do?"

"Well, he stood up by the lake in front of all the other foxes and said, 'Hear me, hear me foxes and foxettes.'"

"Foxettes?" Mrs. Potts asked.

"Don't you worry about that. You know what I mean."

Mrs. Potts chuckled as she went on about her business.

"Now as I was saying," continued Mr. Potts, "the fox without a tail said, 'I have a message for all of you. Here it is in the hot summertime and y'all have to drag around those heavy, bushy tails behind you. Be like me! I cut off my tail and now I'm free. Cut off your tails and you can be free too!'

"'Duh, yeah, sure would be nice not to have tails in this heat,' one of the foxes said and the others quickly agreed.

"The fools were taking out their knives to cut off their own tails when a wise old gray fox who was resting on the other side of the lake yelled, 'Now wait a minute! Don't y'all listen to this fool! I saw him a few minutes ago when he got hung up in a hunter's trap that cut off his tail! He wants you to cut off your tails because misery loves company!'"

"What does that have to do with Gunther?"

"Plenty," Mr. Potts said. "Gunther is not too bright and he won't do the work to make good grades like you. He's miserable and he's trying to make you miserable too. In the same way, that fox that lost his tail in the trap tried to trick the other foxes into doing the same thing until the wise old gray fox got their attention. Some people do the same thing. They try to bring boys like you down to their level. So don't pay Gunther any mind. Leave envious fools like him alone."

A short while later, Lucas' mother arrived and saw Lucas had a bruised jaw. "What happened?"

Lucas explained the situation and Mrs. Potts gave his mother Gunther's home telephone number. "Thank you Mrs. Potts. I'll call Gunther's mother and get to the bottom of this."

Later as Mr. and Mrs. Potts were talking, she told her husband, "Ernest, you do a good job telling those stories to Luke. I hope he remembers them."

"Well, the boy ain't dumb. Too bad other children don't get talked to like that these days. What's for dinner?"

"Fried chicken and, uh, chickenettes."

"Oh, that's nice," Mr. Potts said and thought about it for a second or two. When he realized what his wife said, he turned to her and shouted, "Hey!"

Mrs. Potts laughed then kissed her husband on the forehead.

"Smart aleck!" Ernest Potts muttered as he folded his arms across his chest.

The Fighting Story

It rained that night and the skies cleared the next morning for a beautiful Saturday. That afternoon Lucas stopped by for a visit with Mr. and Mrs. Potts. He was out front dragging a stick through a mud puddle pretending he was using a steam shovel to dig out a canal.

After a few minutes of this, he looked up and saw Gunther Yates.

"Hey, Luke," Gunther said.

"Uh, hello, Gunther."

"You look bored."

"Yeah," Lucas said cautiously. "Nothing else to do."

"Sorry about beating you up yesterday."

Lucas tried to hide a smile, "Your mama whipped you good after hearing about it, huh?"

"Yeah. She said she gonna send me to the juvenile home if I beat you up again, so you ain't got nothing to worry about. Wanna have some fun?"

"How?"

"Come on," Gunther said.

Lucas shrugged his shoulders and followed.

A few blocks away, the two boys passed Patty's Pool

Hall and Juke Joint, which was always busy on a Saturday afternoon. "Come on, Luke, let's check it out!"

"Uh, Gunther," Luke said. "I don't think we're allowed to go in there."

"We ain't. Let's just sit here and watch."

The boys sat on the sidewalk facing the juke joint and saw several men leaving the place. They staggered past the boys slurring their words and smelling like they'd been dipped in a whiskey barrel.

Gunther laughed and Lucas watched wide-eyed.

The drunks stumbled and cursed each other while Gunther howled and Lucas chuckled nervously. Then the town drunk, Frederick Spears, stumbled out the door. "Oh, boy, here's the star of the show!" Gunther said.

Frederick got into a loud argument with the other men in the street. "Y'all don't know who y'all messing with. I am the man! Mister Frederick Davidson Spears the Third!"

One of the other men took a swig out of his bottle of Mad Dog wine, scowled at the town drunk, spat on the street and shouted, "Hey Freddie, if you're really the man, why don't you tell us how to spell that fancy long name of yours?"

"Look here," Freddie said, "I ain't dumb! I've been to Munro's School!"

"Yeah, we know," another one said. "You went there one day, sat in the ditch behind the playground and got plastered."

The men roared with laughter as Lucas and Gunther watched.

Frederick staggered and slurred and held up his finger like he was giving a speech. "When I was a kid, somebody made the mistake of disrespecting my person just like you is doing now!"

"Did he ask you to spell your name too?"

"I choose to ignore that!" Frederick continued. "Yeah, when I was a little fellow, I was up in my front yard helping my daddy move some plants and some kids came along and one of them said to me that I had stepped over in his territory and I had no business there. I says, 'Well, you ain't got no business in my daddy's yard!' To that, the guy balled up his fist and knocked me down!

"My daddy saw it all and said, 'Boy, are you gonna take that?' So I got up and charged like a bull and rammed my head into that boy's belly, and I grabbed him by the feet, swung him around and tossed him like a bowling ball into that gang of his, and they never messed with me no more!"

While Frederick was telling this tale, Ernest Potts was in his tool shed a few blocks away. King White was there perched on a chair. "Hey Ernie, how come you don't hang out with the guys anymore? Things are kind of dull without you and your stories."

"Why do you need me? Y'all got televisions now. Besides, I've been busy. Along with fixing up stuff around here, I've been minding Amelia Moore's boy Lucas. The little fellow looks like he might be somebody when he grows up."

"All that's fine and good," King said, "but you know

what they say about all work and no play. Let's go down to Patty's and shoot some pool."

"I don't drink no more," Mr. Potts said.

"You don't have to drink, you know. Let's shoot pool for old times' sake."

Mr. Potts smiled. "You know, I could stand some recreation. All work and no play does make Ernest a dull boy. Let's go!"

Meanwhile, Lucas and Gunther continued to laugh at the drunkards outside the pool hall. "Better than television, ain't it?" Gunther said.

"Yeah, no commercials!" Lucas said.

Then suddenly Gunther got up and ran. Before he could ask what was wrong, Lucas felt a firm hand on his shoulder. The boy turned and came face to face with Mr. Potts, who was huffing and puffing as he usually did when he was angry. "King," Ernest said to his friend, "you go on without me. I've got some matters to take care of!"

Lucas gulped as the old man led him away from the front of the joint.

"Boy, what were you doing in front of that place?"

"W-W-Well," stammered Lucas, "Gunther Yates took me down there to see the drunks."

The old man shook his head. "Your so-called friend didn't hang around when he saw us coming. That right there should tell you something. Hanging 'round with him is like picking up a rattlesnake and wondering why you got bit. While you're laughing at those drunk fools, those so-called 'men' are making themselves sick and their families poor from wasting their money! Ain't nothing funny about other people's misery."

Lucas let the conversation lapse into silence as they walked to Mr. Potts' house. He thought about what the old man said for a while then asked, "Where was Munro's school?"

"Where'd you hear about that?"

"Mr. Spears said he went to Munro's school."

Mr. Potts smiled and they walked on. "Miss Munro was a white lady who taught around here when they started having schools for colored folks. They liked her so much that they called it 'Munro's School,' although it was actually the Laing School. She was my teacher until they made it illegal for white teachers to teach in the colored schools. Matter of fact, the only time I ever got left back was in fourth grade when somebody accused me of throwing a brick through the school window. Miss Munro spoke up for me, but the school board overruled her and I was left back. To this day, when somebody accuses old timers of not knowing something, we always say, 'I'm smart! I've been to Munro's School.'"

"Oh, so did you know Mr. Spears when he was a kid?"

"Yeah. He's younger than me. He lived with his daddy down the street from us. Frederick says he drinks now because he had it rough growing up, but that's not true. Nobody put a gun to his head and made him drink rotgut. Life is what you make of it."

"How did he have it rough?"

"Well, for one thing, they didn't have too much to eat so he was rather weak. Couldn't fight his way out of a wet paper bag. So the other kids gave him a hard time. One time I saw those kids go into his front yard and beat Frederick up right in front of his father!"

"That's not what Mr. Spears said."

"What did he say?"

"He said he charged them like a bull and whipped them good."

Mr. Potts shook his head. "It's a sorry man who can only be a hero in his own imagination. Sometimes you have to be careful which adults you listen to. Some people love to talk but have nothing worthwhile to say!"

The Storyteller

Mrs. Potts was preparing to hang her laundry on the clothesline in their backyard and Mr. Potts was in the tool shed nearby sharpening some saws when Lucas arrived at the front door.

He rang the doorbell then knocked but nobody answered, so he walked to the backyard and saw Mrs. Potts at the clothesline.

"Luke! Come on back here and help me hang these clothes."

"Yes, ma'am."

Lucas tried to help but wasn't tall enough to reach the line. Mrs. Potts smiled, walked behind the shed and returned with a bucket in hand. She put it under the clothesline bottom side up. "This'll help, Luke."

Lucas stepped up on the bucket and helped her hang clothes. As he picked up a clothespin, he stuck it in his mouth to resemble a duck's bill and began to make quacking noises.

"Boy, take that nasty thing out of your mouth. I swear, you're lucky you weren't a child when I was."

"Why?"

Mrs. Potts reflected on the question and then said, "My granddaddy and me were out by the lodge hall one night, and he and Mr. McKnight were talking. So I decided to look up in their faces to hear what they were saying. Mr. McKnight spit some tobacco out his mouth and accidentally hit me in the eye. I was madder than a wet hen. I looked at granddaddy thinking he would hit him or something. But Granddaddy looked down at me and said, 'That's what you get for trying to listen to grown folks talk!'"

Lucas looked surprised.

"You missed out on some rough times. Now I don't know which is worse, you clowning around or Mr. Potts telling you all those fool rabbit stories."

"Why do you call them rabbit stories?"

She looked at Lucas and a smile returned to her face. "That's an interesting question —and a story in itself. Back during slavery times our folks weren't allowed to learn how to read and write. That's because when you can read and write, you want to do more for yourself than being a slave. So every night, after they were finished working in the fields, they would get together and tell each other stories. Some were about a character known as Br'er Rabbit."

"What's br'er mean?"

"That was slave talk for 'brother.' Anyway, these stories were about a little rabbit outsmarting bigger and stronger animals — foxes, wolves, bears and things like that. Years later a white man down in Georgia wrote a book of rabbit stories he heard from the slaves and eventually somebody made a movie out of it. So telling tales like that became known as 'rabbit stories.'"

Lucas stood on the bucket and continued hanging clothes. "When did Mr. Potts start telling stories?"

"That also goes back to slavery time."

"I thought Mr. Potts was born after slavery!"

"Yes he was and before you ask, so was I!" She chuckled. "Anyway as I was saying earlier, since the slaves weren't allowed to read and write, the only way they could teach each other what they knew was through their stories, and every plantation back in those days had one or two slaves that told stories better than anybody else. One of them was Mr. Potts' granddaddy, a slave named Mr. Jim. Every night after they came in the cabins from the fields, Mr. Jim Potts gathered everybody young and old around him and he'd proceed to tell some of the wildest tales you ever heard."

"Do you know any of his stories?"

Mrs. Potts thought for a moment. "There was one that Mr. Jim passed down to his son, Mr. Jim Potts Jr., who was Ernie's daddy, and Jim Jr. passed it down to Ernie and Ernie still tells it to this day." The old lady stopped hanging the clothes and began to tell the story.

"One night shortly before New Year's Day, old Mr. Jim and all the slaves was coming into their cabins after the master and the overseers had them out working hard all day in the fields. It was already dark because they used to work them from what they called 'Can't see in the morning' until 'Can't see at night.'

"The slaves gathered around Mr. Jim and he was holding forth with tales about masters who were mean to their slaves. One of them walked with a slight limp and talked with a lisp, so Mr. Jim got up and mocked the way that master walked and talked and dragged his own leg to demostrate. The others got a big laugh out of it. They slapped their legs and held their bellies and were laughing, laughing, laughing until suddenly they all stopped."

"Why?" Lucas asked.

"They were laughing so loud, the master heard them and went out to the cabins to see what was going on, and there was old Mr. Jim making fun of how he walked and talked. 'Stop that!' the master screamed, and everybody got real quiet except for old Jim, who didn't hear him cause he was talking and all.

"'Boy, what in the Sam Hill do you think you're doing?' the master screamed.

"Old Mr. Jim stuttered and stammered saying, 'Well, er...ah...uhh,' and everybody was scared for poor old Mr. Jim.

"'Now look here Jim, I don't take no mess from none of my slaves. I got to set an example out of you, so as soon as the sun comes up, I'm gonna have Big Goliath give you a good whipping to remind you who's boss around here!' When the old master left, all the slaves started praying for rain because no whippings were given on rainy days."

Mrs. Potts sighed.

"Who was Big Goliath?"

"Back then, the plantations had certain slaves — usually very big — who carried out the punishments. They often got better food and better treatment than everybody else, which was why they did what they did.

"The next morning, the sun did come up and before Mr. Jim could see well enough to run away, the door to his cabin flung wide open and the master was standing there. 'Okay, Jim. Let's get this over with,' the master said.

"Old Mr. Jim's wife and children and all the other slaves started crying and carrying on as the master tied Jim's hands to his horse's saddle so he could lead him over to the whipping tree. The master looked back at them and said, 'Y'all stop all that noise, or y'all will be next!'

"So, the master got on his horse and led Mr. Jim out to the big oak whipping tree. And he made sure the horse would walk real slow in order to prolong Jim's agony. It was a pitiful sight, that's what Ernie's daddy told him. And Mr. Jim's wife and children were made to walk along behind the horse all the way to the whipping tree.

"When they got to the tree, Big Goliath was standing there waiting. He stood six feet six and was all muscled up. He looked like a huge ebony-wood stump. He held a cowhide whip in his hand, and cracked it now and then to kind of loosen up. The master got off the horse and started tying Mr. Jim to the tree. Goliath spun that whip and was all ready to go and Mr. Jim's family and friends were crying and praying.

"Suddenly they heard the sound of a horse running full speed. Everybody stopped what they were doing and looked, and they saw a soldier wearing the blue uniform of the U.S. Army.

"The master was furious. 'What are you doing on my

property, you blue-bellied Yankee?'

"The soldier pulled out a piece of paper and said, 'Sir, I am here to inform you that this territory has fallen to the Union Army. As such, I must inform you that President Abraham Lincoln has signed a proclamation stating that these Negroes here are now, henceforth, and forever free.'"

Mrs. Potts stopped for a moment and hung the last piece of clothing on the line. She had a sad expression on her face. "Well, so much for the whipping."

Mrs. Potts picked up the clothesbasket and headed toward the house. "What about Mr. Potts' daddy? Did he tell stories too?" Lucas asked.

"Don't know. Ernie's father drowned in a fishing accident long before I came along, so I never met him. Ernie was the oldest of his brothers and sisters, so he took care of the family and went to school. Years later he agreed to take in your own mother when she was a little girl because her parents died. And since he was taking care of everybody, he was the one who did all the talking.

"But here's one he said his daddy told him: You know that big yellow house down the street from the playground? Well back in the days after slavery when things were still bad for the colored people, Ernie's daddy had a cousin named Pete that he was real fond of. One day some crooks broke into a store and shot the mayor's son, who ran the place. The mayor was real mad and walked up and down the street yelling, 'Who shot my son? Who shot my son?'

"That's when one of the crooks started a rumor that

Pete did it. The mayor was so upset that he couldn't think straight and vowed that he personally would hang Cousin Pete. The mayor led a lynch mob to Pete's house, broke down the door and dragged him out into the yard. Ernie's great-grandmother happened to be visiting Pete that day and begged the mayor to leave Pete alone. But the mayor told her to get out of the way because, 'This is a white man's town!'

"So she looked that mayor straight in the eyes and said, 'Mister, the day is going to come when you ain't gonna see nothing but black!'"

"Did they hang Pete?" Lucas asked.

"Yes," Mrs. Potts said. "But Jim Jr. said his grandmother was right."

"How was that?"

"She said that one day the mayor would see nothing but black and sure enough the mayor went blind, and he stayed that way for the rest of his life!"

Mrs. Potts sighed. "Come on, Lucas, help me get this basket of clothes into the house, and be thankful you was born when you were."

As they reached the back door, she added, "You know, it's something to think about. Those folks back then couldn't write down things, so if it weren't for those stories, we wouldn't know anything about our parents and grandparents and the others. So even though Mr. Potts gets on my nerves occasionally with all his stories, he's doing a good thing. Without folks like him, our people would only be names in a graveyard."

"That's how Mr. Potts started telling stories?"

"That's right. Ernie was the first person in his family who went to school, where he learned to read and write. I guess he heard his daddy telling tales, and his daddy heard them from his father. So Ernie was a natural, and when he went to school, he read lots of books about Aesop's Fables and Grimm's Fairy Tales and history and all like that. He still has those books in the tool shed.

"Anyway, Mr. Potts started telling stories that were passed down to him along with the ones he read about. He even made some of them up. That's how Ernie Potts became King of Storytellers around here."

"That's right, and I still got my crown!" Mr. Potts bellowed as he came through the back door.

Lucas looked at Mr. Potts and imagined him sitting on a throne in a big castle, wearing a crown upon his head and telling stories to all his subjects, who were gathered around him listening.

"Shame on you, Ernie," Mrs. Potts shouted. "What you doing sneaking around and listening in on somebody else's conversation, then coming in here screaming and scaring me like that? You gonna give me a heart attack."

"Aw, please!" chuckled the old man as he headed to the bathroom to wash up. "You've been with me all these years and your heart ain't gave out yet, right?"

Lucas smiled.

Later when Mr. Potts was sitting in his big chair in the living room, Lucas came in and sat on the floor in front of him. "Mrs. Potts was telling me about Br'er Rabbit."

Mr. Potts laughed and adjusted his glasses. "Wanna hear one?"

"Yes sir, I would." Lucas said.

"Once upon a time, Br'er Rabbit and Br'er Fox was in love with the same girl — a real wildcat, I'm told.

"She lived in a little cabin down by the creek. It's important that you remember where she lived, OK?"

"I will."

"So one evening Br'er Rabbit was sitting out on the front porch with that gal and she says, 'You know something Br'er Rabbit, you're kind of cute, but Br'er Fox is handsome.'

"'Well thanks a lot!' Br'er Rabbit said real sarcastic like.

"'Now don't get mad, Br'er Rabbit, there is one way you can win me over Br'er Fox.'

"'How's that?'

"'Show me that you're smarter than Br'er Fox and I'll be yours.'

"Br'er Rabbit looked kind of confused. Then he says, 'OK, baby, I'll see you around,' and left the cabin wondering how he was going to prove he was smarter than that fox."

Lucas' eyes widened as Mrs. Potts walked in from the kitchen wearing a knowing grin.

The old man continued, "So the rabbit went by the fox's cabin to see what he could see. He looked into the window and saw Br'er Fox looking at himself in the mirror. He was combing his fur and saying, 'I look too good! I am so sharp that I'm afraid I might cut myself. Ha!'"

Lucas burst out laughing.

"So anyway, the rabbit started banging on Br'er Fox's door and he said, 'Who's there?'

"Br'er Rabbit opened the door and hopped in on one leg like he had a limp.

"'Greetings and salutations, Br'er Rabbit. Something wrong with your leg?'

"'Well, you see Br'er Fox, I hurt my leg real bad and I need a favor — I need to go down by the creek tonight but I can't get there on this bad leg.'

"'What's that got to do with me?' Br'er Fox asked, knowing full well that the beautiful wildcat lived down by the creek.

"'Well, I was going to ask the donkey to give me a ride out there tonight. But he's feeling mighty poor too, so I was wondering, could you give me a lift?'

"'What? You want me to mess up my beautiful fur just to take you down by the creek? I shan't do it!'

"So Br'er Rabbit said, 'If you do this for me, I'll let you know the next time the gate is open over at the chicken coop.'

"If there is one thing that foxes love, it's a fat chicken for supper," Mr. Potts explained.

"So Br'er Fox said 'OK.'

"Br'er Rabbit hopped on the fox's back and off they went to the creek. And after a little while, Br'er Rabbit said, 'Br'er Fox, please do me another favor.'

"'What is it this time?'

"'I sure do miss the way that the donkey would kick up

his legs and holler hee-haw, hee-haw whenever he took me for a ride. You mind doing the same thing?'

"The fox said, 'Br'er Rabbit, you have completely lost your mind! I shall never stoop so low as to do such a foolish thing!'

"'Don't forget, Br'er Fox, I will let you know when the chicken coop is unlocked.'

"That's when that fox kicked up his back legs and yelled, 'Hee-haw, hee-haw!' as loud as he could while the rabbit was holding on tight.

"Well, all that racket made that girl sit straight up in her bed. She got up and said, 'Sounds like that fool donkey is done got loose again! How does he expect anybody to sleep with all that hee-hawing going on?'

"So she walked over to the window of her cabin and looked out in the yard.

"'Oooh-wee!' she exclaimed as she saw Br'er Rabbit out there riding Br'er Fox like a cowboy busting broncos in a wild-west rodeo.

"'Ya-mule! Giddyap!' Br'er Rabbit hollered, and that fox was kicking up his legs and screaming, 'Hee-haw, hee-haw!'"

Lucas laughed so hard he was crying.

"Don't you know, that girl stepped out on her porch and said, 'Br'er Fox, I swear you are the stupidest thing on God's green earth! What you doing out there kicking up such a fuss with that rabbit on your back? I don't want no fool like you hanging 'round me!'

"Then she walked over and grabbed Br'er Rabbit by the

hand as he slipped down onto the ground. 'Come on, Br'er Rabbit. It's time to see the preacher man!'"

Lucas rolled on the floor laughing, and Mr. Potts said, "You see, Luke, back in the old days, the slaves told their children stories like this for good reason. The only way they could beat the system was not with their fists. It was with their brains. Don't ever forget that, and you'll do just fine."

With that, the old man sent the boy off to do his homework. As Mr. Potts began to read his newspaper, he heard Mrs. Potts clapping in the kitchen.

"You trying to get smart with me again?" the old man asked.

"No, Ernie," she replied. "That was a great story. It was so good, in fact, that I decided to throw away our television set."

"Yeah, right," Mr. Potts chuckled.

The Shrimp Monster

On a pleasant Saturday around midday, Mr. Potts finished sawing some two-by-fours he needed to repair a wall in the tool shed. "The best thing about being retired is I can quit work whenever I want to," he said to no one in particular as he wiped the sweat from his brow. Then he headed inside for lunch. Mrs. Potts had promised to make him a cheese sandwich, which was there on the kitchen table along with some sweet iced tea when he came through the back door.

Upon finishing his meal, Mr. Potts turned to Lucinda and said he planned to take a walk in the park.

"That's nice, Ernie. I'm going to the church in an hour for a meeting with the sisters."

Mr. Potts kissed her on her cheek and promised to be home early for supper. Mr. Potts strolled the sunny streets on his way to Alhambra Hall Park. He passed Pierates Cruze Gardens where he worked as a lawns keeper as a young man. The beautiful flowers along with the clear sky and the singing birds reminded him of the simple pleasures of nature.

After arriving at the park, he sat on a bench and fed

the squirrels some pecans he brought with him in his coat pocket. He heard a group of children playing nearby. As he looked past some trees, he saw Lucas playing with a group of other children, including Gunther Yates.

"Say Gunther, bet'cha I can do something you can't do," Luke said.

"Like what?"

"See that house over there?"

"What about it?"

"Well, I'm gonna take off my shoe and jump over it."

The other children laughed as Gunther replied, "Ain't no way you can do that! Nobody can jump over a house!"

Mr. Potts wondered exactly what trick Lucas had up his sleeve.

"Just watch," Lucas said as he bent down and untied a shoe. The children stopped laughing as Lucas removed his left shoe and placed it just right on the ground. He pointed it toward the house. The children watched in eager anticipation as he stepped a few feet back and ran toward the shoe, which was pointed at the house. As he got closer and closer, the girls in the group began to hide their faces and Gunther broke out into a cold sweat.

Lucas ran as hard as he could and jumped clean over his shoe, then bent over to catch his breath. Gunther ran up to him and shouted, "What's up with that? You didn't jump over the house!"

"I didn't say I would," Luke replied. "I said, 'See that house over there,' and that I'd take off my shoe and jump over it. I didn't say nothing about jumping over no house!

Come on, Gunther, even you've got better sense than that!"

Gunther took serious offense to Lucas' little trick. "You think you're slick!" Gunther said. He balled his right hand into a fist and cocked it back and said, "I ought to...."

But somebody had walked up behind Gunther and grabbed his arm before he could let Lucas have it. "What the...?" Gunther shouted as he spun around and faced Mr. Potts' stomach. "Uh, hey Mr. Potts."

"Look here, Gunther," the old man said as he turned his arm loose, "that boy didn't lay a hand on you. Besides, Lucas is a whole lot smaller than you. So I suggest you leave him be, and carry yourself on home."

As Gunther and the other children left, Natasha Washington waved to Lucas and smiled as she joined the others. Lucas ignored her, sighed in relief and said, "Thanks, Mr. Potts."

"Don't thank me," he said as he sat down on a nearby bench. "If I weren't here just now, Gunther would have whipped your behind. It's good that you stood up for yourself, but be very careful about tricking people like that."

Moments later he looked at Lucas and asked, "You ever hear the one about the Shrimp Monster?"

Lucas smiled as he shook his head.

"There was these two little sisters — Tina and Nina. Tina was the oldest, and a little on the stingy side. Anyway, their mama was frying up a batch of juicy shrimp and Tina said, 'MA-ma, can I have some?'"

Lucas laughed and noticed that other people were gathering around the park bench to hear the story.

The old man continued, "So the mama said, 'Of course you may.' Tina sat down as happy as could be with that plate of juicy fried shrimp.

"Then Nina asked, 'TI-na, can I have some shrimp?'

"Like I said," continued Mr. Potts, "Tina was rather stingy, so she told Nina, 'You don't wanna eat this shrimp!'

"'Why not?'

"'Because when little girls like you eat shrimp, scary things happen.'

"Like most little kids," Mr. Potts noted, "Nina got real excited about the possibilities and asked, 'Like what?'

"'Well,' Tina obliged, 'when a little girl eats shrimp and goes on to bed later, she gets a pokey feeling in her stomach — poke-poke, poke-poke — and suddenly her stomach bursts wide open and out steps the Shrimp Monster!'

"As Nina shook in terror, Tina curled her hands like a monster's claws and added, 'He's gonna come after you and say with a deep and scary voice, 'You have eaten me so now I will eat you!''"

Mr. Potts continued in an animated fashion. "So Nina cried 'Wahhhh!' and their mama came running in the room. She dried the little girl's tears and asked, 'What is the matter?'

"'Tina told me that th-th-the Shrimp Monster would gobble me up.'

"'Oh she did, did she?' her mother said, then spanked Tina's behind. 'And for scaring your sister like that, Tina, you're going to bed right now!'

"So Tina went off to bed upset and angry. She fell asleep

and soon afterward she had an odd feeling in her stomach — poke-poke, poke-poke!"

Lucas smiled.

"Next thing you know, Tina heard a roar and an ugly creature burst out of her stomach."

Mr. Potts crossed his eyes and made a horrible face as he continued. "That big ugly beast said in a deep voice, 'You have eaten me, now I will eat you!'

"'Waahhhhh!' screamed Tina, and her mother ran into the bedroom. 'What's the matter?'

"'MA-ma, the Shrimp Monster is after me too!'

"'Well,' her mother said, 'that's what you get for scaring your little sister.'"

Lucas laughed as the old man concluded, "You see, Luke, the old folks say that you reap what you sow. In other words, if you go around playing tricks on people, don't be surprised if a nasty trick happens to you, too. It's called irony."

Everyone who had gathered around the bench to hear Mr. Potts laughed and applauded. "Great story, old-timer," somebody said. "Got any more?"

Mr. Potts was embarrassed a little as he tapped Lucas on the shoulder and said, "Come on, boy. Let's go home."

War Stories

After arriving at the Potts' home one afternoon a few days later, Lucas went straight to the table and pulled out his books and note pad.

Mr. Potts put down his newspaper and asked, "About to do some homework, Luke?"

"Yes, sir."

Then the doorbell rang. It was Lillian, Mr. and Mrs. Potts' daughter. She held a package under her arm as she walked into the house.

Mother and daughter embraced, and the old man stood up and said, "How's my 'cute little self' doing these days?"

The woman smiled, "Still cute but not so little anymore, Dad." She chuckled while looking at his belly and noted, "Mama is feeding you well."

Lucas observed all of this with mixed emotions. He admired the closeness of the Potts family but missed his own father.

"Anyway, Mama," Lillian continued, "Roscoe and I will celebrate our anniversary next week and I need your help with this dress pattern."

Mrs. Potts agreed and the women headed to the sewing

machine in the den.

"So what did you say your homework was about?" Mr. Potts asked Lucas.

"The Second World War."

"Now that's a huge assignment. I lived through it, and it was tough."

Luke knew another story was about to commence.

"After I finished school, I worked a while as a gardener at Pierates Cruze. It was hot out there in the sun, I'll tell you. So I decided to get some more schooling at the Colored Normal Industrial Agricultural and Mechanical College of South Carolina up the road in Orangeburg."

"The what?"

"South Carolina State College for short. But in those days, it had that long name because they taught black kids how to teach, build things and grow crops. That's where I learned how to use my tools. My daddy had drowned in a fishing accident a few years before that, so I worked my way through college as a waiter in the dining hall. It was called Floyd Hall, and my colleagues sang a song about it that went like this:

> *Floyd Hall Boys are we*
> *We're just as happy as we can be*
> *Oh those biscuits in the oven*
> *How I wish I had some of 'em*
> *Floyd Hall Boys are we!*

Lucas laughed so Mr. Potts sped up the tempo and

clapped his hands in time. "Get up and dance, Luke, if you want to." So he did.

> *Floyd Hall Boys are we*
> *We're just as happy as we can be*
> *Oh those biscuits in the oven*
> *How I wish I had some of 'em*
> *Floyd Hall Boys are we!*

The old man concluded in a deep bass voice: "Hall Boys are weeeeee!"

With that, Mr. Potts joined Lucas and they both danced. Mrs. Potts and Lillian heard all the noise and peeked through the doorway. Mr. Potts turned around and stopped cold when he spotted them.

His smile disappeared. "Don't you two have something else to do?"

"We do," Mrs. Potts replied.

"But this is more fun," Lillian added.

The old man huffed and puffed for a moment then turned to Lucas and continued the tale.

"Anyway, I didn't get to finish college, but I married Mrs. Potts and worked as a carpenter for a dozen years until the war started. I was checking the mail one day and saw a letter addressed to me from President Franklin D. Roosevelt himself. 'Greetings,' he wrote.

"That was his way of saying 'You done been drafted.' So off I went to war.

"After I got my basic training at Fort Jackson in Columbia, I was transferred to Camp Croft in Spartanburg, which was fine because it wasn't too far for Lucinda to come see me now and then. Then they sent me down to Georgia, not far from Savannah, to Hinesville. Back then everything was segregated. There were white regiments and colored regiments — just like with everything else. When we ate in the mess hall — that's what they call a cafeteria in the Army — the white cooks refused to serve us. So our major tells the cook, 'Hey! Serve the colored troops just like you serve the white ones.'

"The head cook then said, 'Oh, all right. I'll serve them.'

"So we got some scrambled eggs, but when we started eating them we looked at each other and said, 'Why are they so crunchy?'

"Turns out that the son-of-a-gun scrambled the eggs shells and all!

"So the major ran up to the cook and hollered, 'I told you to serve these men a proper breakfast!'

"Then the head cook grinned and said, 'Yes, sir, but you didn't say how!'"

"Excuse me, Mr. Potts," Lucas said, "how come the white people treated y'all so mean?"

The old man pondered the question a moment as did his wife and daughter, who were still listening in. Mr. Potts regained his composure and continued.

"A long time ago our great-great-grandparents were brought here from Africa as slaves. Before that the folks used poor whites — they called them 'indentured servants' and native Americans — they called them 'Indians' — to do the work around their places. But that didn't work too good because all the poor whites and Indians had to do was run away to be free. There were lots of other whites and Indians they could go to back then. But since the black folks were from Africa and didn't know the land, it was easier to keep them in bondage. They really didn't know where to go if they took off from their masters.

"But the white folks who were running things worried that if the Indians, poor whites and black folks ever got together, they wouldn't be in charge anymore. So they tricked members of each group into hating each other. That way, the rich white folk maintained control over the masses. You'll understand this a lot better as you get older, Luke, so before we get too deep into the subject, there's something I want to make sure you understand. Are all the black people you know good and smart?"

"No, sir." Lucas thought about Frederick Spears and Gunther Yates.

"Are all black folks evil and ignorant?"

"No." Lucas thought of his parents, Mr. and Mrs. Potts and Valerie.

"So, are all the white folks you know at school ignorant and mean?"

"No, sir. Mrs. Sanders was real nice to me in first grade. She gave me books and let me perform in school plays."

"Well, then, are all white people good and smart?"

"No."

"That's right, Luke, always remember that no matter what some folks tell you, good and evil don't come in colors."

Lillian and Mrs. Potts looked at Ernest with pride for such a profound answer to Lucas' question.

"Now back to the war. After that business with the mess hall, they shipped us out to Iowa. We were stationed near a small town, and one night we were allowed to go off the base. So there we were out with our uniforms in the middle of nowhere where they probably never saw nothing black but shoe polish. We saw this guy sweeping in front of his store and decided to go inside to get something to eat. The man was skinny and wore thick glasses. When he saw us coming, he dropped his broom, ran in the store and locked it up tight!"

"But Mr. Potts," Lucas asked, "if people treated y'all so bad, why did you fight for them?"

"Because we believed that if we proved ourselves as good soldiers, things would be better for black folks like my daughter and you someday."

"How could y'all stand all those 'white and colored' signs all over the place?"

Mr. Potts took Lucas over to the picture window. "See that telephone pole in front of the house?"

Lucas nodded.

"Have you ever stopped to think about it being there?"

"No, sir."

"Why haven't you noticed it?" asked the old man.

"Because I see it so often that I don't think about it."

Mr. Potts smiled. "That's how it was with us with all them segregated signs back then. We saw them so often that we didn't think about them very much at all."

"How did you figure all this out, Mr. Potts?"

"Two things: By living and by reading those books I have in the tool shed."

This answer satisfied Lucas so Mr. Potts resumed the narrative.

"When we left the United States, we were shipped out to Saipan, off the coast of Japan, to fight the Japanese. Boy, them Japanese weren't playing when it came to war! If they captured you, they'd give you the water torture. They'd tie you to the ground and slowly drip water on your head. I don't know why, but after a few hours of that, you felt like they were dropping hammers on you."

Mr. Potts paused for a minute. "Say boy, I thought you were supposed to be writing all this down."

Luke quickly broke out of his trance. "Oh yes, sir," he said as he grabbed a pencil and some paper.

The old man resumed the tale. "But you know, there was one thing the Japanese troops wouldn't do to us. Some Japanese soldiers out there in the South Pacific would actually eat the white soldiers when they killed them. But they would not eat us. See, the Japanese, like a lot of people in those days, thought that we weren't as good as the whites. That was one time I bowed my head and said, 'Thank God for prejudice!'"

Everyone got a good laugh at that one.

"But something happened back then that really affected my future. I was taking my final exams for college by mail. I had all my papers ready to go back to America to finish my college degree. But the Japanese invaded our post and the papers were burned.

"But please remember this: If you throw a duck into water, it either sinks or swims. That's how you ought to look at life. Only the strong survive so don't be too upset about what happened way back when. You should keep on going until the day you die.

"Anyway, after that raid, everybody was all shook up. One night I wanted to ask my sergeant something and for no reason, he threw a knife at me. Good thing I knew how to duck! I wondered how I was going to get out of that place alive! But a few months later, I was playing tennis on a makeshift court, and they told us the war was over. We'd be shipping out soon! I got down on my knees and said, 'I know I'm going to heaven because I just came back from hell! Praise God from whom all blessings flow!'

"So as soon as my ship came back into the port in Charleston, I took the bus over to Mount Pleasant and boy was my family glad to see me."

The old man smiled at this memory. "I got a job at the shipyard after that, and even invented a caulking device that made me some extra money. That lovely lady over there had that cute little lady next to her a year later."

His wife and daughter beamed. Mr. Potts asked Lucas, "Think that'll make a good homework paper about World War II?"

Lucas was at a loss for words.

Mr. Potts continued, "There's one thing I want you to add in that paper — it's something I want you to remember more than anything else. When I got back from that mess in Saipan, I was a happy man. I saw how bad life can really be sometimes. It takes things like that for you to appreciate it when times are good. Do you know what the word 'tragedy' means?"

"It means like a big disaster, like a house fire in which people are killed."

"Good. Do you know what an inconvenience is?"

"Something bad that's kind of minor, like dropping an ice cream cone in the dirt."

Mr. Potts smiled. "In this life you should know the difference between a tragedy and an inconvenience, and fact is, you can't be happy if you've never been sad."

A Pretty Good Day

Mr. Potts sat on the porch reading his newspaper and enjoying a steady breeze when Lucas arrived a few days later. As the boy ran up the porch steps, the old man asked, "Well Luke, how'd everything go in school today?"

"I got an A on my paper about World War II. I even added some stuff about Jackie Robinson and Joe Louis."

"That's nice," Mr. Potts said, and noticed the wind blowing the leaves. "It's a nice day today, too. Do you know what we used to do on days like this?"

"What?"

"We flew kites. Wanna give it a try?"

"Sure, Mr. Potts. We can buy some kites at the drugstore. When Mama comes, I'll ask her for some money."

"Oh no, boy, save your money. Come with me to the tool shed. I'll show you how to build one."

In the tool shed, the old man gathered some glue, sticks and paper and patiently instructed Lucas on how to build his own kite. They finished about a half-hour later and walked to a grassy hill behind the playground.

"Here's what we'll do, Luke. I'll hold on to the body while you let loose the spool of string. When you let out enough string, start running. I'll let go of the kite and let the wind take it away!"

"Sounds good," the boy said as he unwound the string. Moments later Mr. Potts yelled, "OK Lucas, the wind is starting to blow just right, so start running."

Lucas took off down the hill and the kite lifted into the air.

"There she blows!" Mr. Potts said.

Lucas ran faster and faster and as he looked up, the kite was twirling up and away.

"That's right, boy! Keep running. Up it goes! Faster! Faster!"

Lucas ran faster as the kite went higher and higher until it seemed to touch the blue sky. "Yeah, boy!" Lucas shouted.

He slowed down to a stop and held the string tight as the kite held steady in the sky. Then Lucas walked back up the hill to where Mr. Potts launched it. But as he got closer he saw Mr. Potts was down on his knees clutching his chest. He coughed and huffed like he used to do when he was smoking. "Help me up, boy. Once I'm standing up straight again I'll be OK."

Lucas stood firm as the old man grabbed him at the shoulder and pulled himself back to his feet. "Very good, Herbert Lee, stand still while I get my balance. Yes, I'm all right now. Let's go home."

"Why'd you call me Herbert Lee?"

Startled, Mr. Potts turned his head away from the boy and looked off into the clouds.

"Isn't that the name of your son who was killed?" Lucas asked.

Mr. Potts' eyes grew almost to the size of golf balls. "Who told you that?"

"Mama did, a long time ago."

Mr. Potts scowled. Lucas figured he said the wrong thing. The old man coughed hard twice then explained. "Herbert Lee had just started at South Carolina State in Orangeburg and was back home for the weekend. He'd been working on Mingo Hodges' ice truck whenever he was home to make money for school."

"What's an ice truck?" Luke asked.

"Oh yeah, you're kind of young to know about that. Back before people had refrigerators, they kept their food cold in wooden iceboxes. There was a shelf down at the bottom to hold a big block of ice. The ice was delivered to people's houses in an ice truck. Anyway, Herbert Lee was in the back of the truck and Mingo was driving, and they came around a sharp curve on Mathis Ferry Road and Mingo lost control. The truck hit a tree and…."

Mr. Potts sighed and put a stick of gum in his mouth. "…And that was the end of Herbert Lee Potts."

Lucas knew better than to ask anything more at that point, so he started winding up the string on a short stick and the kite slowly came down.

"Fine boy, he was. Real smart. Liked to follow me around and listen to my stories. I taught him to fix stuff, too. I always hoped that one day he'd pick up where I left off."

After the kite landed on the hill, Lucas put the string in his back pocket, picked up the kite and followed Mr. Potts back to the house. They weren't too far from home when Lucas asked, "You don't like talking about this, do you?"

"Do you like talking about your father?" Mr. Potts asked.

"Not really."

Mr. Potts put his arm around the boy and calmly said, "I can understand that. Back during the war when I was stationed up at Camp Croft, I went to Mount Moriah Baptist Church. There was this old lady there named Mother Minnie Montgomery. She was born just after slavery ended. No matter how bad she felt, whenever somebody asked her how she was doing, she'd say, 'Fine, just fine.' A lot of folks my age are like that. We don't like to bother other people with what's bothering us. Maybe we should talk about these things more often."

They stood in silence for a while before Mr. Potts smiled and said, "Speaking of your daddy, Robert told me a story about you."

Lucas noticed the leaves blowing in the breeze. "Really?"

"Remember the old Sears store on St. Philip Street in downtown Charleston?"

"Oh yeah! They made candy right in the store and they'd give you some as you came in through the front door. I liked the orange gum drops the best!"

"That's right, and they had an escalator that you liked to run up and down. It tickled me how the country people would gather around at the bottom and wonder where the steps went as they disappeared into the floor."

Lucas laughed and Mr. Potts went on, "Anyhow, Robert

said that when you were three years old, he took you to Sears, and while you were waiting in line on the second floor for him to pay his bill, there was a lady with a great big behind that was almost sticking in your face."

Lucas laughed. He felt good that Mr. Potts thought he was old enough to listen to that kind of comment.

"You were a little fellow and didn't know any better, so you reached up and patted the lady on her backside, and, well…" Mr. Potts choked out the words amidst his laughter, "she turned around looking really mad at Robert and reared back and was about to smack your daddy in his face with her purse right there in front of everybody.

"So Rob took your hand and smacked it and said, 'Boy, what did I tell you about doing things like that?'

"So the lady, realizing that it was you who patted her and not your daddy, stormed off without saying another word."

Mr. Potts was walking sprightly now as they laughed about the tale.

Another gust of wind blew and the old man watched the glow of the setting sun across the landscape as they arrived in front of his house.

"Luke," he said, "overall, this has been a good day, hasn't it?"

"Yes, sir."

"Just think about it, the sun looks as nice as it does, you got a good grade on the paper and then we flew the kite — one you made on your own — you should be very proud of yourself."

"Thanks, Mr. Potts."

"Not every day is going to be like this, boy."

"What do you mean?"

"You're going to have some really bad days too. So remember, when you do, think of days like this because life is good."

"I don't get it."

Mr. Potts sighed. "Trust me, one day you will."

Lucas packed his books and headed out the door to his mother's car when he realized he had forgotten his manners. He turned around and yelled, "Hey, Mr. Potts? I'll see you tomorrow."

The old man looked at Lucas, paused and replied wistfully, "You sure will."

Not After All

After an ordinary day at school, Lucas started out for the Potts' house. But as he approached it, he noticed his mother's car parked in the front, which was very unusual. He also noticed Mr. Potts' daughter, Lillian, and Valerie getting out of their car.

As Lucas entered the house, he was puzzled to see the old man sitting upright in a dining room chair in the middle of the floor, his bald head shining under the light of a lamp. His glasses were gone and he had a huge white sheet over his shoulders as if he was about to get a haircut. The women took turns helping him.

Lucas walked up to where the old man was sitting and said, "Hey, Mr. Potts."

But he did not respond. He simply shifted his eyes toward Lucas. He tried to say something but nothing came out.

"What's the matter Mr. Potts? Cat got your tongue?"

"Lucas," his mother said as she wiped a clean towel across the old man's mouth. "Now is not a good time to bother Mr. Potts."

Mrs. Potts and Lillian opened a jar of baby food, and

Mrs. Potts started feeding her husband.

"Mr. Potts," Lucas asked, poking the older gentleman on the arm, "why is a grown man like you eating baby food?"

"Lucas Moore, that's enough!" Mrs. Moore shouted. "Go find something else to do, right now!"

Lucas was about to cry when Valerie took him by the hand and led him outside.

"What's going on?" he asked her.

"Granddaddy had a stroke last night, which means something bad happened in his brain."

"Ohhh," Lucas said, "How long is he going to be like that?"

"Nobody knows. All we can do is try to keep him comfortable."

"What can I do, Valerie?"

"For the time being, just go upstairs and do your homework."

Valerie's soothing voice calmed Luke down a little. "Maybe later on we can go for a walk," he said to her.

"Sorry, buddy. I should stay around the house to help with granddaddy while he's sick."

"Oh well," Luke sighed and went upstairs.

• • •

"Lucas, wake up!" Mrs. Moore said as she shook Lucas. "What's the matter, Mama?"

"I just got a call from Mrs. Potts."

"What happened?"

"Mr. Potts passed away."

Lucas sat up straight, but said nothing.

"Lucas? Do you understand? He died in his sleep," she said.

Lucas nodded, remaining silent.

"Lucas, do you want to talk about this? I know this is so hard for you...."

"Not yet, Mama," Lucas said with tears in his eyes. "Maybe tomorrow."

• • •

Over the next few days, preparations were made for the funeral. As was the custom in Southern black neighborhoods, the community brought lots of food to the Potts' residence. Mrs. Moore allowed Lucas to attend the visitation at the funeral parlor. Aside from a simple goodbye, Luke had little to say about the passing of his friend and mentor. This worried his mother.

"You have to understand," Mrs. Potts explained to Amelia, "children Lucas' age find it hard to say what they're feeling at times like this."

"That's what worries me," his mother said. "I wonder what's going on in his mind. I'd hate for him to bottle up all of his emotions. It's not good."

"He'll be all right. Just give him time. Everybody deals with these things differently."

Later, Amelia had another talk with her son as they sat on the sofa. He was reading a book that Mr. Potts had given him.

"Son, how do you feel now that you've seen Mr. Potts' body?"

The boy turned a page of the book without looking at

his mother. "I'm glad I got to say goodbye."

"That's good, Lucas. I wanted to talk to you because I think it's best that you don't go to the funeral."

"Why not?"

"Well, some people get very emotional — crying and whooping and hollering — and it's not a good idea to upset young children with all of that stuff. So if it's OK with you, I'd like for you to stay at the Potts' house with the other children. Valerie will look after you, just like she did when you were little."

Lucas put the book aside, turned on the television and said, "OK."

Amelia looked on in concern.

The funeral took place the next day. It was a lively service. The choir sang a lovely rendition of "By and By" and everybody in the church clapped and sang. The pastor and many of the town's residents testified about all the good things Mr. Potts had done over the years.

After the burial, Amelia joined everyone else at the Potts' house for a family gathering.

"Well, at least that part of it is over," she said to Mrs. Potts.

"Yeah," Mrs. Potts said, "the town folk showed how much they appreciated him."

Mrs. Potts chuckled.

"What's so funny, Mama?" Lillian asked.

"Knowing the old man as well as I do, he's jumping up and down on a cloud up there madder than a wet hen asking, 'How come they didn't give me flowers while I could still smell them?'"

Everyone in the room laughed.

"But sure enough," Mrs. Potts said, "Ernest did do a lot for people in this town. I'll even miss his fool rabbit stories."

"Yeah," Lillian said, "what is this town gonna be like without the old man?"

Everyone shook their heads sadly and some even began to cry. That's when Valerie walked in. Amelia asked, "How's Luke?"

"Y'all aren't gonna believe this. Come with me into the den."

The adults looked through the door. Luke was standing in the middle of the room while the children sat all around listening.

"What happened after that?" Gunther asked.

"Mr. Potts said that once the war was over, he was glad to get back home and start a family, which he did. But you know what? He said he learned a lot while fighting for our country."

"Like what?" Gunther asked.

"Mr. Potts said that you can't be happy if you've never been sad."

Mrs. Potts turned to all the adults and whispered, "Well I'll be! The old man ain't dead after all!"

The End

About the Author

Damon Lamar Fordham was born in Spartanburg, SC on December 23, 1964 to Anne Montgomery and was adopted in September 1965 by Pearl and Abraham Fordham of Mt. Pleasant, SC, where he was raised. He has appeared on numerous radio and television programs on South Carolina Educational Television and British Broadcasting Company's Radio 4 and has written for many magazines and newspapers. A graduate of the University of South Carolina, he received his MA in History from the College of Charleston and currently teaches history at Charleston Southern University, Springfield College at Charleston, and Virginia College at Charleston. His other books include *True Stories of Black South Carolina* and *Voices of Black South Carolina*.